RHYTHM

MARIE LIPSCOMB

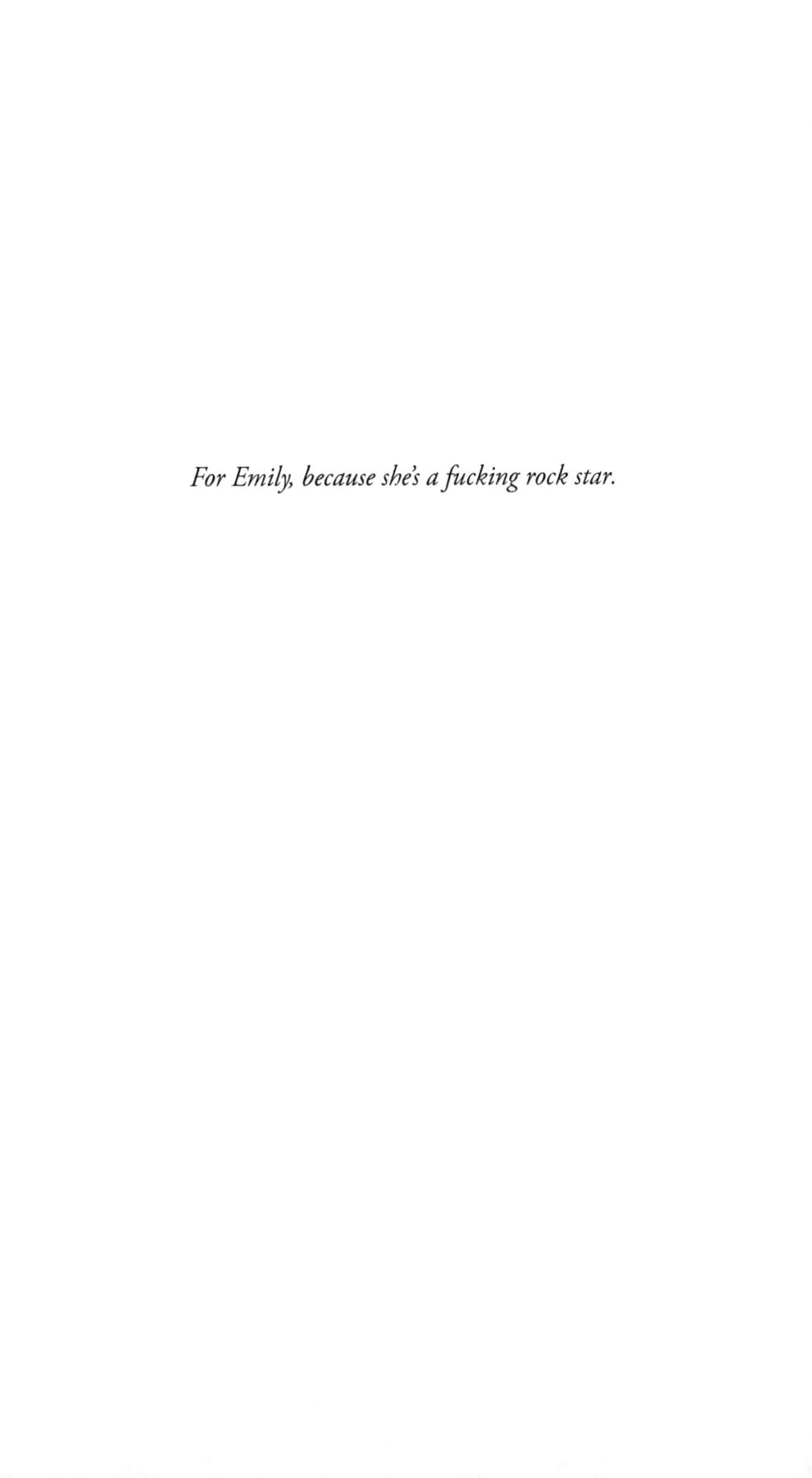

For Emily, because she's a fucking rock star.

Rhythm

ONE

Beth's bones rattle as she's thrown around by the uneven road and slammed against the jeep's door. Actually, *road* is too generous—it's more like a track blasted out of the side of the mountain and leveled using a crazy straw. The knuckles on her right hand are bloodless as she clings to the door handle.

Beside her, her friend Sadie frowns in the driver's seat. She shifts gear and struggles along the potholed track. Her warm, tawny brown complexion pales at a particularly expensive sounding *thunk*.

"Are you sure this is right? I have a terrible feeling about it." Sadie shoves her long, silky, straight black hair back from her face, not daring to take her eyes from the path ahead. "And I don't like the look of those clouds over there. Looks like rain."

"I can handle rain."

"This whole situation is sketchy."

With her free hand, Beth scrolls through the listing on

her phone, reading the *how to find us* section of the booking. "I'm positive it's this road. They do say it's pretty bumpy."

"Bumpy is an understatement."

"I'm sorry…"

"For the record, I still think this is a ridiculous idea."

"Ridiculous ideas are my forte."

Sadie taps her manicured matte-black nails on the steering wheel as the ground evens out to something resembling a driveway, and gravel crunches beneath the jeep's tires. "Do you still have signal?"

"Yep. And there's Wi-Fi in the cabin too. If I need you, I'll call or message you."

"And what if an axe murderer cuts the power?"

"Sadie…"

"Beth?"

Beth shakes her head, the thick brown waves of her hair spilling over her shoulders as she sighs and turns toward the window. Trees pass by slowly as they creep along the track, and she catches sight of her pale white face in the window's reflection. Dark shadows hang beneath her eyes. How long has it been since she slept longer than four hours? The exhibition's deadline is fast approaching, and every day she's more and more convinced her inner critic is right; she's a fraud.

Sure, she can draw and paint, but she's no artist.

Picking at a thread on the cuff of her jacket, she tries to push aside her negative thoughts. She needs this break. She needs to get away from the city, from the noise and stress.

A long weekend retreat in a remote cabin, all by herself in the mountains. Nothing to distract her, no one around for miles, no car, so she can't bail when things get too difficult. Just her, the beautiful country, and her art. And it *is* art.

If she can concentrate, if she can produce something

meaningful, then maybe it'll be deemed worthy of the gallery.

Sadie huffs at her side. "I just don't feel good about leaving you up here all by yourself."

She has always fretted over Beth, ever since they met fifteen years ago in school. Almost immediately she had fallen into the role of the older, sometimes-annoying, always-lovely sister Beth always wished she had.

"Alright Beth, I'm serious. Call me every morning and every evening, okay? If I don't get a call, I'm heading up here with the cops… and the army."

Beth chuckles. "There's no one else up here. What could possibly happen?"

"Bears." She glances at Beth, her eyes wide and eyebrows nearly up to her hairline. "Snakes. Bears wielding snakes as weapons. Snakes commanding an army of bears."

Folding her arms over her chest, Beth plasters an over-exaggerated scowl on her face. "You think I can't defend myself against a snake-wielding bear?"

"I know you *think* you can defend yourself against a snake-wielding bear. That's what worries me. Please, please, *please* don't do anything stupid up here. 'Kay?"

"Yes mom."

Sadie rolls her eyes. "Elizabeth Barlow, if I was your mother, I'd put you over my knee."

"Don't threaten me with a good time."

Sadie shakes her head and laughs as the road curves and the cabin comes into view. Beth's heart lifts at the sight of it. Sliding glass doors on the top story, lead to a small wooden balcony looking out over a majestic view of the mountains. The cabin itself is every bit as picturesque and lovely as the images online, but with one pretty major pitfall. The big, beat-up black van parked outside somewhat spoils the scenery.

Sadie sighs. "Oh, joy. Now that's a murder van if ever I saw one."

"Wait…" Beth furrows her brow as she scrolls through the booking again. Her stomach churns. "Someone's already here?"

"Maybe it's the owners?" Sadie parks the jeep beside the van and cranes her neck to look at the phone.

Beth's scrolling becomes frantic. With every passing moment, her dream of solitude is slipping away. She finds the email from the cabin's owner, and reads it again.

"No, it says here they left the key in a lockbox on the side of the building. I have the code for it. It's definitely not the owners." She exhales sharply and rubs her eyebrows with her thumb and forefinger. "Fuck. Maybe they've double booked it."

"You're positive this is the right cabin?"

Beth squints at the sign hanging from a Narnia-looking signpost out front. "Foxglove… yeah." She quadruple-checks the booking. "It says here "Foxglove-upper."

"Upper?" Sadie arches her eyebrows.

Beth frowns. "There were no other turns. This has to be it."

If this whole thing was a waste of money and an hour-long drive up a mountain side, she's going to… well probably just moan about it to her friends and politely ask for a refund, but still… grr. This was her chance for peace.

"I'll call the owners," Beth grumbles. "See what's going on."

Paradise. The shower cascades over Finn like a scalding monsoon, melting the tension and ache in his shoulder muscles. He'll be sore tomorrow, but he'd expect nothing less. The ache means he worked for it.

With a contented sigh he rubs pine tar soap across his broad, hairy chest and under his armpits. He keeps his eyes screwed tight against the rivers of suds sliding down from his hair.

Getting away from the city to focus on his work was a good idea. No, a great idea.

In the five days since he arrived at the cabin, he's made great progress. He could happily spend the remaining nine days in the shower, hot water blasting his aching body. But he can't. There's always work to do, and he's come a long way for solitude.

His hands slide over his soap-slick skin, his body hair helping to work the suds into a thick lather. It's pretty handy like that. His own personal loofah.

He rubs both hands over the soft, hairy mound of his stomach, as he rinses his hair and beard, holding his breath beneath the torrent of water. He'll get back to work in a second.

But it's Friday. No one would blame him for taking a day off. He could explore a bit, go out and see the mountains and the ancient pines growing a short hike away from the cabin. Every year he tells himself he'll explore the area, and every year he locks himself away and works. He's sure there must be eagles or some other cool animal he can find.

No. He has to make the most of this. When will he ever have this much time completely alone? No neighbors around to complain, no noise curfews.

Pushing his face out of the stream of water, he takes another gulp of air and goes back under. The water pelts the back of his neck like a thousand tiny stones. It's almost painful, but he's a big man; he can take it. Inspiration always comes when he's in the water.

Pressing his palms against the slate tiles of the shower wall, he drums out a rhythm with his fingertips, nodding his head in time with the song thundering through his mind. It's good. Feral. But he needs to get out and test it, check whether it sounds as good once he's plucked it from the symphony hall in his brain.

Most things sound better in his head, both music and words.

Turning off the shower, he grabs a thick, dark blue towel and wraps it around his waist. He uses another to dry his hair and torso, and takes time to moisturize the black, scrolling tattoos on his arms. It seems kind of pointless now. He's all clean and pine scented, but within moments he's going to be hot and sweaty. At least by the time he's through playing, the water tank should have had time to refill.

He pulls on a pair of boxers and a fresh pair of faded blue jeans. With the rhythm still pounding through his head, he grabs the first clean shirt he finds. Like so many of the other shirts he gets for Christmas and birthdays, it has Animal from The Muppets screaming wide-mouthed from his chest. The words "Me like drums" are emblazoned across his belly. His mom bought him that particular shirt. It's a size too small, but the sentimental value makes up for it. She was trying. He's pretty sure he could put together an entire outfit of nothing but Animal merchandise well-meaning people have gifted him if he searched through his closet.

"Right." His hands are already twitching, desperate to get

started. He sighs contentedly as he walks back to the living room, to where his pride and joy is set up, taking up a quarter of the space.

Over the years he's tweaked and personalized her; a custom paint job, new pedals, new skins, extra drums and cymbals. Now she's twice the kit she was. She's a thing of beauty, and as he stretches his arms, holding them one at a time over his chest and relishing the strain of his muscles, he can't wait to hear her sing.

Two

"Beth, are you really sure about this? I'll drive you back to town. It's no problem."

Beth rolls her eyes as she reaches the top of the wooden staircase running along the side of the cabin's exterior, weighed down by her backpack. Not to mention the rolled canvas containing brushes, a toolbox of paints, and the stack of canvases and paper beneath her arms. Ever since the mortifying call with the very sweet and elderly-sounding lady who owns the cabin, Sadie has been on her case.

She should've figured it out from the name alone; Foxglove-upper. Only the top floor of the cabin is rented to her. The bottom half—presumably Foxglove-lower—is rented by someone else. Not quite total isolation, but still a far cry from the bustling city.

Beth punches the code into the key safe and retrieves the little silver key nestled inside. "It was my fault. I should've known when this place was so affordable. It's fine. I'm sure we'll barely even see each other."

"Yeah, well I'm sure they'll be counting on you not being

able to see them while they're creeping around the woods at night trying to watch you through the windows."

"Wow, Sadie."

Beth sets her stuff on the floor by the door and forces a weary breath. The cabin is lovely, every inch of it meticulously designed to be as comfortable and inviting as possible. Almost everything is made of wood, except for the massive cream-colored corner sofa, and the brushed steel kitchen appliances. The sliding glass doors at the other end of the cabin give her a perfect view of the mountains and misty late-fall forest below. There's a small, spindly wooden table and two chairs set out on the balcony, ready for an idyllic, if cold, breakfast for two. Yeah, there's no way she could've afforded somewhere like this without a catch.

"What if it's a man?" Sadie huffs as she carries Beth's easel into the cabin and glances round, trying—but failing—to mask her approval of the cabin.

"What if it is?"

"Well, what if he's a jerk… or a murderer."

Beth's eyes widen as she claps her hands over her cheeks and opens her mouth, a gesture mimicking Edvard Munch's *The Scream*. "What if he's a jerk *and* a murderer?"

"You're such an ass," Sadie sighs. Her smile fades as she looks around the cabin. "Please be safe. I don't want to have to go on a quest to avenge you."

"Yeah not again. The last one was pretty messy. One and done."

Sadie rolls her eyes. "Call me, assface."

"Seems a little harsh, but I'll respect your wishes, Assface."

Beth braces herself for a retort as Sadie grimaces and looks at her watch. "I'd better make tracks. I want to be back in civilization before night. I'll be back on Sunday evening to rescue you. Don't get murdered. 'Kay? No bears. No men. No snakes."

"I'll try."

"Love you. Call me." Sadie steps outside and begins her descent of the stairs.

"Love you too, stop fretting. Just get home safe."

The door closes, and Beth is alone. As she waves Sadie off from the balcony, she can finally breathe deeply. The rumble of the jeep fades, and her mind begins to turn. She pulls in a deep lungful of the fresh mountain air, and listens to the… well… the silence. Blissful.

Already, her mind is adventuring, inspiration pouncing on her, as though it followed her through the deep, dark woods. She wants to paint— paint the silent mountains, the soaring eagles, the imagined dangers lurking in the forest below. It's going to be her best work. She can feel it. Clouds hang heavy and low above the mountains, shutting them off from the rest of the world.

Her entire body flinches as thunder rolls through the air. Thunder which keeps rolling.

Standing perfectly still, Beth listens. The sound is coming from below. A pounding, earth-shattering rhythm, primal, savage. It's definitely not thunder.

Her heart plummets. "Are you fucking kidding me?"

Drums. It had to be fucking drums.

Finn loses himself to the rhythm, throwing his heart into every thundering beat. The ache in his arms doesn't matter. The sweat pouring down his body can be washed away. This is his masterpiece, his magnum opus. Vixen's Wail has been teetering on the brink of making it big for years. He's going to send them over the edge, careening into the Rock and Roll Hall of Fame.

Fuck yes.

But the rhythm is suddenly off kilter, another beat pounding out of time with him. He stops, gripping a cymbal to stop it from shivering.

Someone is beating the door. His heart drops as he stands. Five days. Five blissful days of making as much noise as he wants, thrashing out his frustration on the drums, and now there's someone in his space. It's the off-season, the soggy part of fall where all the golden foliage is just brown mush on the ground. There shouldn't be anyone there. There never has been before.

He strides over to the door, pulls it open, and the sight which greets him is like a punch to the gut.

A woman, short and curvy, and absolutely heart-stoppingly gorgeous. She has thick, wavy brown hair and furious eyes. She's beautiful, but holy shit is she mad. The glower she casts over him, trailing the length of his torso, before returning to his eyes, hollows his chest.

"Hi… Hey…How's it going? Can I help you?" He dabs the sweat from his brow on the back of his tattooed forearm and tries to come off as nonchalant, leaning against the doorframe.

"Hi," she forces a smile. Her voice is deep and smooth. She probably sings really well, or could, if she ever learned. "I'm staying upstairs for the weekend."

"Oh." He presses his lips together and waits. She seems to think that's enough, that she doesn't have to tell him why she's there, and to be fair, she doesn't. He knows exactly why.

But he's not giving up his practice time without a fight. "And?"

She chuckles incredulously. "And your drums are really loud."

"Yeah, I know. That's why I come up to the mountains to practice."

She nods slowly, glancing to the side and pursing her lips. "Well I came up here for the quiet."

"Oh… okay then." He raises his eyebrows, braces his elbow against the doorframe and presses his knuckle to his temple. "Well, I don't know what to tell you. I have work to do."

Her eyes harden as she stares back at him, and in an instant he knows he's met his match.

For a moment, Beth forgets why she even came downstairs. The man looks down at her, his eyebrow arched quizzically. His thick forearms are almost completely covered in black tattoos so she can only make out slivers of tanned skin between the ink. He's tall, but the breadth of him puts him in proportion. The biggest drum kit in the world would look like a kid's toy with him sitting behind it.

But the sight of him quells her ferocity.

The lazy, self-assured way his eyes drag across her figure, stoke twin fires of excitement and indignation, their flames flickering in her chest. When he leans against the doorframe, she's a little afraid it'll buckle beneath his weight. The muscles in his arms strain against the sleeves of his tight, black shirt; a Muppets shirt, which clings to his rounded belly and broad chest.

He's so big, so burly. But—she reminds herself— so fucking noisy. She tries very hard to focus on unappealing aspects of him; a loud, sweaty, obnoxious drummer who wears an Animal shirt. A walking stereotype.

"I can't concentrate on my work with you pounding away down here."

He grins at her unfortunate choice of words. "Oh?"

"Can you maybe keep it down?" she says, her treacherous voice growing huskier in his presence.

Could you maybe pound me instead?

What the hell, Beth?

He sighs deeply, crossing his arms over his big, broad chest. "I'll try."

Her cheeks prickle with heat as his lips curve into a smile. Of course, he has an irritatingly attractive smile. Seriously, fuck this guy. "Thanks."

"Alright. See you." He closes the door, and her breath comes back to her in a rush of cold air. Silence descends on her like an avalanche.

"That wasn't so bad." She smiles and heads back up to her floor, careful not to let her feet thump too hard on the wooden staircase. A small part of her feels guilty for asking him not to play, and if it were any other instrument, she might not have said anything, but drums... no. She can't work with that. A long weekend with a professional kazoo player would've been preferable to the thundergeddon he calls music.

She treads lightly when she gets to her floor, refusing to give him any opportunity to complain about her noise. That's okay. The quieter the better.

Once her easel is set up, and old sheets cover the pristine floorboards, she's unstoppable. She paints a forest of trees with branches reaching out like tendrils. Eyes peer through the shadows as a monster, a behemoth cloaked in shadow, skulks through the background, disrupting the peaceful forest with its overbearing presence. It's not exhibition-worthy, but it's something—more than she's managed in over a month. She calls it *The Beast Below.*

Already exhausted, she cleans off her brushes and makes her way to the bathroom. Turning on the shower, she slips out of her clothes while she waits for the water to warm up. So far, so good.

THREE

Finn's fingers twitch against the arms of his chair. His foot taps out the rhythm as his eyes trail across the ceiling, following the clunk and creak of her footsteps. The whisky in his glass is nearly gone, but he holds onto it, swirling the ice cubes around for something to do.

This is ridiculous. He paid to be here, just as she did, and yeah, his drums are loud, and alright, the way he plays them they're really, *really* fucking loud, but he has as much right to do what he wants in the cabin as she does. The water pipes groan above and her shower hisses. Okay, so he's either going to have to shower with cold water, or go to bed dirty. Perfect. Just perfect.

A sigh escapes his lips. He's restless and grumpy, and he can't get the rhythm out of his head. He could drum for a couple of minutes while she showers. He'll be as quiet as he can be.

Once the silencing pads are in place on the drums, and his cymbals are covered with mutes, he shoves some rubber tips on the end of his sticks and begins. It's nowhere near satisfying, but it helps him burn off energy, helps get the beat out of his brain and into the world. It doesn't take long before his skin is shining with sweat again, and his calf is cramping from working the pedals. He grits his teeth and plays through. He has to improve his stamina. Neil Peart would power through, and so will Finn Tovey.

The fiery whisky still stings the back of his throat as he grits his teeth and growls. Summoning his last scraps of energy, he builds to a crescendo that could shake the mountains. But his heart misses a beat at the sharp knock on the door.

"Oh shit." He stands, his legs trembling beneath him, and hurries to answer it.

The woman is standing there in the fading light, her hair soaked through. She wraps her long coat around her body, fitting it to her curves. Her legs and feet are bare and reddened by the heat of the water and what must've been a purposeful march down the steps. The floral scent of her shampoo wafts toward him, clenching his throat.

"I asked you not to play." Her teeth chatter in the cold.

For one wild moment, he has an urge to pull her to him and keep her warm. His mind taunts him, telling him she's naked underneath the coat, letting him imagine what her soft body would feel like against his.

He clears his throat and braces his forearm against the doorframe. "Uh. No, you asked me to keep it down."

"Well I can still hear it."

"This is about as quiet as I can make it. I have pads on the drums, mutes on the cymbals, rubber tips on the sticks. It sounds like garbage, but we're just going to have to deal."

Her throat twitches as she looks to the side incredulously, as though she has a whole heap of suggestions at her disposal right next to her. "No, I can't *deal*. I can still hear it. I need to sleep. Can you just not play?"

A laugh shakes his chest. She may be pretty, but she's rapidly becoming a pain in his ass. "Listen—"

"No, you listen," she snaps. "I'm tired, I need to work tomorrow. I have an exhibition coming up and I need to concentrate."

Heat flares along his neck. Man, he hates conflict, but he'll be damned before he backs down on this. He compromised, after all. "Well I'm on tour next month, and I need to practice. It's only, what? Like, eight thirty anyway. No one needs to go to bed this early."

They stare at each other. Her cheeks flush pink, and he can't help thinking if she blushes that way when she fucks.

Damn, he really is an animal. "What's your name?"

"Why do you want to know?" She hesitates for a moment, her face hardening as she regards him. "Beth. You?"

His lips form the shape of her name, leaving the tip of his tongue pressed to his top teeth. He clears his throat and shakes her out of him.

"Finn," he says, leaning against the door frame, and hoping to disarm her with a smile.

And for a moment, he thinks, it might have worked.

Fucking Finn. Finn-fucking-tastic.

Any longing Beth had for him has long gone, replaced by annoyance and frustration. He didn't really deserve to be snapped at, but she's freezing her tits off, wearing nothing but her coat—which was a terrible idea, but she was so pissed off she couldn't think straight—and she can smell the whisky on his breath. He's a big, drunken oaf.

"We need to come up with a compromise. I'm here till Sunday and I don't want to spend the whole time telling you to be quiet." She shakes her head, and beads of water drip from the tendrils of her hair. What was she thinking?

"Alright." He flashes her a lazy, half-smile. "Do you have headphones?"

"Yeah—"

He leans toward her, his eyes soft. "So, use them and stop disturbing me, Beth."

The door clicks shut and she's left open-mouthed, trying to process what happened. "Just keep it down, okay?"

She drags herself up the stairs, her heart racing a little as the first raindrops begin to spatter. Confrontation always gives her the jitters and she never handles it well. A hundred iterations of the things she should've said flash through her mind, each one more cutting than the last

When she gets back up to her floor, she trudges to the bedroom, finds a pair of thick socks to warm up her feet, and puts on her pajamas. Her phone flashes on the nightstand; a missed call and a text from Sadie, which reads: *Are you dead??*

After a few moments of deliberation Beth types out her response:

This is an automated message, sent by the ghost of Elizabeth Barlow. The loud, obnoxious (but weirdly, kinda cute) DRUMMER staying downstairs annoyed her to death. Please remember her fondly.

She hits send, and a heartbeat later the phone vibrates with an incoming call. Sadie's name flashes across the screen.

Beth slides her thumb across to answer. "Yup?"

"He's cute?" Sadie's voice sounds a little distant. The phone signal might not be so good after all.

"Yeah…like in a big lummox kind of way. But he's a drummer, Sadie."

"Hmm…yeah…rhythm…stamina…how terrible. Tell me more."

"Stop," Beth laughs as she curls up into the corner of the L-shaped sofa, scraping her wet hair back. "He's noisy, and obnoxious, and we're already archnemeses."

"You yelled at him?"

"I didn't yell, I just told him to be quiet… a few times." She glances up as the wind howls outside. Rain taps against the roof, already forming waterfalls over her balcony. She loves storms. If not for her downstairs neighbor, the whole scene would be thoroughly Pinterest-worthy. "Apparently he's on tour soon and he needs to practice."

"Tour?" The pitch of Sadie's voice raises an octave. "So, he's like… big time? Professional?"

"No idea. I've never seen him before. Tour could mean moving from his mom's garage to his friend's garage for all I know."

"What's his name?"

"Finn… are you looking him up?"

"Yup." After a slight pause she sighs. "There are thousands of Finns. Surname?"

"Don't know. He has a beard and a bunch of tattoos on his big doofy, muscly arms. And he likes The Muppets."

"Ooh… I have to see him. I'll get searching."

Beth laughs. "I'm sure you have better things to do."

"Beth, Beth, Beth. It's like you don't know me at all."

"Alright. Report back with your findings."

"Agent Sadie, over and out."

The call ends, and Beth sits with a bemused smile, still clutching her phone. The urge to join Sadie in her hunt for information is tempting. Already the beast below is occupying an uncomfortable number of her thoughts. Even if he is handsome, any chance of romance probably ended when she demanded he stop playing.

Her smile dissolves as the muted, rhythmic tap of his drums begins again.

Sadie's assumptions about his stamina proves true. On and on he plays, tapping away for hours, only stopping for torturous moments of silent rest before the noise starts up again.

By the time the sky is ink-black and he finally stops, she doesn't dare to hope. But the silence in the cabin is only punctured by the clatter of plates and cutlery below, and the low drone of his microwave.

"Thank you, Finn, you asshole," she whispers as she crawls into bed.

She stares at the ceiling, picking out patterns in the grain of the overhead wooden beams, searching for faces in the dark spots, as the threat of the gallery's deadline keeps her from sleep. By the time her brain switches off long enough for her to drift off, the sky is already growing bright again.

FOUR

I t's still raining when Finn wakes up the next morning, as though the world is telling him to stay inside and practice. He checks out the front window and though he can't remember what her vehicle looked like, there's only his van parked out front. Either the woman upstairs has given up and left, or she's out exploring one of the little towns at the foot of the mountain. Both options suit him fine.

He brews his coffee and pours a cup, topping it off with a splash of cream, and a teaspoon of sugar, (because life is short and he loves himself) while he looks over the sheet music he wrote last night. He barely slept, working long after he stopped drumming, figuring out the riffs on his old electric guitar, headphones in, obviously, so he didn't disturb her. He isn't a complete asshole.

"Looking good," he whispers, smiling as the coffee touches his lips.

It's already 7 a.m. If she's gone for the day, he'd better get in as much practice as possible. Gleefully, he takes the silencing pads off the drums, frisbees them onto the couch and sets the cymbal mutes on the table behind him.

"Time to make some noise," he grins, slipping the rubber tips off the end of his sticks.

A flurry of confusion which quickly boils over into rage propels Beth from her bed. She's barely even awake by the time she's leaping down the stairs. Beast-mode activated. It's time to kick some drummer-boy ass.

The rain is coming down in sheets, and a shallow river gushes down the side of the mountain, covering the gravel driveway. She doesn't give a shit about the rain. Her fists ache as she thumps the door. "Are you fucking serious?"

He can't hear her. Of course he can't. If the mountain suddenly erupted, the noise coming from his floor would drown out the blast. She presses her face against the window, and a smidgen of her anger shifts into lust.

Power. That's what it is. His muscular arms are shining, sweating and taught. His eyes are clamped shut, his brow furrowed, and lips parted as he lifts his head, back arching a little, his big body shaking with the rhythm. It must be what he looks like when he—

No. Stop. Don't think that. He's an ass.

But ugh. Fuck, I wish I was that drum kit.

She shakes away the ridiculous thoughts and bangs on the window, cringing a little at her own lack of self-control. It's a wonder her fist doesn't go straight through the glass.

He looks up with a start and damn near drops his sticks. "Oh fuck," he mouths.

"Yeah, oh fuck. You bet your fucking ass oh fuck."

The door rattles, and in an instant Finn's body fills the frame, chest heaving as he fights to catch his breath. "I thought you'd gone out."

"I was asleep!" The threat of tears stings her eyes. The rain is soaking her through, and her hair clings to her face.

The scent of salt and pine, and heat of his body, wafts against her as he cranes his neck out the door, scanning the driveway. "Where's your car?"

"I don't have one."

"Oh." He pauses, and a smug little smile crosses his lips. "So where did you park your broomstick?"

Despite herself, she laughs. "Just around the corner, propped up beside the bridge I assume you usually live beneath."

"Ouch." His eyes travel from her shoulder to her eyes, leaving a scorching trail. He holds her gaze for a moment, before he chuckles and glances back down at the torrent of water gushing past the cabin. "That's a lot of rain."

"I don't care about the rain. I just want to sleep and work in peace."

His eyes pass over her as she folds her arms over her chest, suddenly all too aware that she came down in her white cotton pajamas, no bra, no shoes. Shit, he can probably see everything.

***

Finn tries his best not to stare, but it's hopeless. He can see everything, and his pants are growing uncomfortably tight. Her nipples are hard, pressing against the fabric of her pajamas. White pajamas, and little shorts, becoming more and more transparent by the second.

Don't look. Do not look.

"Listen," he says, staring above her head at the peaks of the mountains in the distance. "I have to work. If I don't get these songs written—"

"I have to work too."

They're arguing in circles and it's doing neither of them any good. If either of them are going to get anything meaningful done, they need to compromise, perhaps alternate between a noisy hour for him, and a quiet hour for her. It seems as fair as anything.

He's about to suggest it when she pulls her phone out of the pocket in her shorts. Her brow furrows as she swipes away a notification. "What's Vixen's Wail."

"My band…" He's taken aback. Is she…did she look him up? "How did—"

She turns on her heel and heads back toward the stairs, her round ass looking thoroughly biteable in her little frilly shorts.

"Please just shut the fuck up," she calls down as she climbs.

Confused, and uncomfortably turned on, he retreats inside, listening to her stomp on the floorboards above.

FIVE

"Okay," Beth sighs into the phone as she shuts the cabin door behind her and stands by the heating vent to warm up. "Spill."

Sadie cackles triumphantly on the other end of the phone. "Good morning to you too. He's the drummer for a band called Vixen's Wail. They're a symphonic metal band."

As she grabs a towel from the bathroom, she notices how transparent her shirt has gotten in the rain. Great.

With a grimace, she turns on the shower and leaves it to warm up. "That's… actually pretty cool."

"He's the only guy in the band. There are seven members; your drummer boy, five women, and their violinist who's non-binary."

"Find me something to hate about him," Beth instructs as she switches to speakerphone and starts to undress, wrapping herself in a towel while she waits for the shower. "Is there like a bio or something? Photographs of him kicking puppies? Anything."

In the silence her mind starts to whirr. She heads into the

living room and sits on the sofa, pulls her sketchbook onto her lap and starts to draw.

Her jaw clenches as the noise starts up below, muted but still audible. *Tap tap taptaptap. Tap tap taptaptap.*

She rolls her eyes as Sadie's voice comes from the speaker. "Is that him I hear?"

"Yeah. He puts these rubber pad things on the drums to make them quiet." She frowns as she sketches, and it isn't long before the image becomes clear. It's him, eyes screwed tight in furious concentration, his hair disheveled as though someone has already run their fingers through it.

Sadie gives a short, sympathetic laugh. "*That's* the quietened down version?"

"Exactly."

"I can see why that would be annoying, but honestly, he sounds pretty good," Sadie says. "Ah… okay. It looks like he's dating the singer. And she's fricking gorgeous."

"Oh—" She tries not to sound disappointed, but she's not at all convincing. "Well that settles—"

"Wait. No. He *was* dating her. They broke up but they're still good friends and write all their music together. Yeesh."

Yeesh indeed. A good relationship with his ex, probably means he's a decent person, which in this case, is extraordinarily inconvenient. She keeps sketching, adding a pair or vicious boar tusks to his bottom teeth. "Keep going. There must be something."

"Nothing I can see. He seems like a nice guy…but there are pictures. Oof… he has no shirt on here." Sadie chuckles on the other end of the phone. "Damn, that's a lot of boy. You're right. He is cute. Maybe I'll just happen to knock on the wrong door when I head on up there to pick you up…I can come now if you like?"

"No." The possessiveness in her tone startles her. She distracts herself from Sadie's laughter by shading a pair of curling, satanic horns coming out of his head.

"You've got it bad, haven't you?"

As Beth releases a breath, she's frustrated to find that Sadie is right. When she thinks of him her stomach flops. She almost wants to keep going downstairs to complain so she can see him again, and the thought of him, shirtless, sweating, is…honestly, it's turning her on. "I'm going to put some music on, try to drown him out, and get some work done."

"Call me with updates. I want to know when it happens, I want all the gory details. Length, girth, positions, everything. Got it?"

Beth draws a sharp breath and forces out a sigh as she disconnects the call.

How does she know about Vixen's Wail? And what's she planning to do with the knowledge?

Finn scours the forums on his band's website, looking for shitty comments from a new user, but if she's on there she isn't saying anything. In the bottom corner of the screen, he can see there are four members online, and one guest. Perhaps that's her.

She's chattering away upstairs, probably on the phone to the cabin's owner, complaining about his antisocial behavior. She's in for a surprise when she does, but he'll probably still get his ear chewed off. His grandma is proud of her cabin, and her near-flawless five-star reviews.

The reviews. His blood runs cold. Beth can complain to

him all she wants, but if she messes up Gigi's average and her overall rating dips below a 4.9 because of him, he'll never hear the end of it

With a sigh, he throws the silencing pads back on his kit and starts to play, softly, carefully, trying not to disturb her.

If I piss her off enough though, maybe she'll come down again in those see-through little pajamas.

He tells the voice in his head to shut up, but plays a little harder regardless. He can't quite shake the image of her ass jiggling as she ran up the stairs.

An-i-mal! An-i-mal!

The fantasy of her haunts him, filling his head, pushing out the music, the rhythm, the beat, until there's nothing but her. He closes his eyes and imagines her knelt between his knees, her nipples pressing against the sheer, wet fabric of her pajamas, her full lips wrapped around his cock, slowly stroking him to climax.

He opens his eyes and pushes out a breath. This is ridiculous. He needs to get her out of his head.

He stops drumming, lays his sticks down, and heads off to the bedroom, cock so hard it aches. She's nothing more than a distraction. A prissy, sexy, annoying, gorgeous distraction, and damn, does he ever want her. He lies back and uses both hands, one cupping his balls, the other tugging at his cock as he imagines her trying to keep him quiet by sitting on his face.

His breath shudders as his rough hands grip his sensitive cock. He wants her, wants her softness, her tender touch, wants to hear her voice shatter until all she can do is whimper. What he wouldn't give to make her come.

Rolling onto his stomach, he bucks his hips against the mattress and uses the friction of the sheets to get himself off.

He buries his face in the pillows, pretending they're her thighs, imagining her hot little pussy beneath his tongue. Each thrust brings him closer.

"Beth," her name leaves his lips like a wish, stifled against the pillows.

———

The music blasting out from the Bluetooth speaker drowns out Beth's gasps.

"Oh, shit." She sucks her breath between her teeth as her little bullet vibrator buzzes against her clit. Pressing her head back against the pillow, she can see stars, lost in the rolling waves of pleasure as her toes curl, and her climax builds quickly.

His tongue. His hands. His cock. She wants him all. She imagines him standing at the end of the bed, her feet pinned to his shoulders as he thrusts into her. Her hands all over his stomach and chest as he teases her clit with his calloused fingers.

"Fuck… Finn…"

Her thighs shudder as she comes. A ragged, almost-pained cry escaping her lips as her pussy pulses beneath her hands. Immediately oversensitive, she turns off the vibrator, tosses it back into her bag, and lays back, basking in the afterglow of pleasure.

Her music is turned up loud, and that's how she'll keep it. If he wants noise, he'll get it. Silence would have been preferable, but music comes with the added bonus of pissing him off. Occasionally, she can listen to instrumental music as she works, nothing with lyrics, and for now, definitely nothing with drums. Fuck drums. Fuck Finn.

Climbing out of bed, she straightens out her clothes and heads into the bathroom. The shower has been running ever since her conversation with Sadie, and the mirror is completely steamed up. "Oops."

With a grimace she switches it off. She'll shower later. For now, she'll paint. The monstrous portrait of Finn snarls at her from the sofa, as if he knows what she just did while thinking of him. Even as a drawing with tusks and horns she wants him. In fact, if she's being honest, the tusks and horns are pretty hot too.

A sharp knock at the door raises the corners of her lips into a grin. She stands completely still before her easel, brush poised to paint.

"Beth?"

The way he says her name, so sharp and commanding sends a thrill through her body. Her cheeks are still flushed, and as she saunters toward the door, she wonders if he'll figure it out.

He arches an eyebrow as she opens the door, and her music blasts out to meet him. Cold air and harsh morning light rush into the cabin. It's still raining, hard.

"Really?" He has to yell over the blasting music.

She gives him a one-shouldered shrug and smiles. "'Sup?"

His cheeks are flushed, almost as red as hers, and his bottom lip is sucked pink. He has clearly made some attempt to slick back his hair, but it's unmistakably tousled. Her nipples tighten as she lets herself imagine he was touching himself too, thinking about her. She's going to need more batteries before this weekend is over.

"Listen," he huffs. "I need to shower, but all the hot water has gone."

"Oh." The rhythm of her heart kicks up. "Yeah, that was me. My bad. I switched it on and kind of forgot about it."

His eyebrows shoot up a little at her admission. "Alright, we share a tank, so please be considerate."

Considerate? Heat flares along her jaw. The man who awoke her at the ass-crack of dawn with thundering drums, is preaching consideration to her. The urge to tear him a new one rises in her chest.

"And please turn your music down." He blinks as the rain batters him. "I made my drums as quiet as I could. I'm making compromises. You're just being loud for the sake of it now."

He's right, and she knows she's being petty, but nevertheless she grins. "I thought you like noise?"

"I like my noise. Yours is… what is this?"

"Music," she shrugs. "It helps me think."

"You can't possibly work with it turned up this loud."

"It's better than listening to your awful drumming all day."

His face hardens. "Awful?"

"Yeah. It is. Have you ever sat and listened to nothing but drum solos for hours on end—?"

"Yeah?"

"—No, because everyone knows drum solos suck. I don't want to listen to it."

He recoils a little, his eyebrows furrowed. "Why don't I come in and take a look at your art and tell you everything that sucks about it? Music is my art."

Beth scoffs. "Art?" Her heart lunges against her ribs as she stares him down. "There's nothing remotely artistic about that noise. A chimpanzee could do it."

She expects anger, retaliation, but he's silent, and in a way it's worse. If she was a fraction less stubborn, she'd apologize, but she's tired and cranky, and it's his fault entirely.

The way he stares at her, hard-eyed, undaunted, unyielding, sends lighting prickling along her skin. She braces herself, half expecting—and half hoping—he'll slam her up against the wall.

Finn's lips part. "Are you serious?"

"Yes. It's just mindlessly hitting things. It sounds absolutely terrible."

A huff of bitter laughter bursts from him. He shakes his head and raises his eyes to the dark, rainy sky. She's wounded him, deeply, but she doesn't feel victorious, not in the slightest. Guilt creeps through her ribs like a vine, its thorns pricking her heart.

Finally, he speaks. "You want to be this way? Fine."

As he turns and stomps down the stairs, cold dread trickles down her spine. She didn't mean it, any of it, but he's hurt, and she can't stand to know she caused his pain. "Alright, I'm sorry. I'll turn the music down," she calls after him, but he doesn't break stride. "Shit."

The door beneath her slams, and moments later the air erupts with ear-splitting thunder.

Six

D*ude, stop. You're being absurd.*

Whatever. She wants mindless noise he'll give her mindless noise. Finn picks up his sticks and begins thrashing out a rhythm, louder and harder than he's ever played. His legs are still jelly from jerking off, his feet soaked from stamping through the waterlogged earth, but it only adds to the effect, making him hit the bass pedal a beat out of time.

She doesn't like it when he plays well, and she sure as hell won't like it when he plays bad. He drums and drums, skipping from one rhythm to the next, a little Nightwish here, a little Vixen's Wail there. It's erratic and awful, and he's even giving himself a headache.

He screws his eyes shut and drowns out the world. There's no cabin, no Beth, just him, the music. And the water.

There's water splashing up his leg.

"Fuck!"

He leaps up from the stool and grabs his bass drum and pedal. There's already an inch of murky floodwater and brown leaves on the floor, and it seems to be rising pretty quick.

"Oh shit."

He's panicking, his heart racing as he scans the room. Did she somehow flood the tank when she left the shower on? Is she doing it?

He runs to the entrance at the back of the cabin, blood running cold as he's faced with the deluge spilling down the mountainside and beneath the back door; a flash flood.

"Oh shit. Shit shit shit."

He has to rescue the kit. No matter the cost, even if it means…

Stomach dropping, he glances up, to the now-silent floor above.

"Ah…" he hisses as the inevitable becomes unavoidable. "Shit."

<hr>

Beth opens her door, head pulsing, eyes watering. "I'm sorry. You win. I'll leave in the morning."

"No time. Grab this."

Her eyes widen as he thrusts an enormous drum into her arms. "What—"

"My floor's flooding. I need to get these out of the water. Can I keep them here?"

Pulse quickening, she sets the drum inside as he takes off running downstairs. Her thoughts can hardly keep up as she follows him. Water is gushing all around the outside of the cabin, from the looks of it, at least a foot deep and still rising. Her feet thud against the wooden steps, as she calls out for him, "Finn?"

As she reaches the bottom and wades around to the front of the cabin, the full extent of the flood becomes apparent. Water sprays out from the door, rushing down the road, carrying sheets of paper and leaves. Finn's panicked footsteps splash loudly inside.

"How can I help?" She steps inside as the freezing water laps at the ankles of her pants. "What should I carry?"

"Cymbals. Those things there." He points as though she doesn't know what a cymbal is.

There's no time to be huffy though. She grabs one in each hand and carries them by their stands. Hurrying through the rain, she runs upstairs as he follows behind, carrying a stack of three drums. They set them inside before he turns back to the door.

"There's still more." He's panting, his voice strained with panic.

"Why do you have so many drums?" She calls out as she follows him back down the stairs.

"Compensation, obviously."

Despite her panic, she bites back a laugh as they load themselves up with more drums and cymbals and hurry up the stairs. The whole kit sits in the middle of her living room, dripping wet and unsightly. They take another frantic trip back down and load up with two guitars—one acoustic, one electric—an amplifier (which Finn declares is "probably fucked anyway"), a wad of sheet music, and a keyboard.

When all his instruments sit in a pile, safe on the top floor, he growls in frustration and rakes his fingers through his hair. "This is just perfect."

"Can we call someone?"

"Who? The flood police?"

"I was thinking mountain rescue, smartass." She takes

out her phone, and her stomach drops as she notices she has no signal at all. "Shit."

Finn takes out his phone and frowns. "Yeah. Mine's dead too. The rain must've knocked the signal out." His eyes widen and his lips part. "Oh crap. Clothes."

He takes off running down the stairs, leaving her standing by the door. Her heart races as her mind grasps at a solution. They can't call for help, and he can't stay down there in a flooded room. He'll have to spend the night there, sharing the top floor with her.

She can almost hear Sadie cackling.

SEVEN

To say he feels guilty is an understatement. In a little over twenty-four hours, he's kept Beth awake late, woken her early, jerked off thinking about her, pissed her off more times than he can count, and now he's invading her space. It's not even 9 a.m.

Her floor is bigger than his—taller, anyway, with a steep, pointed ceiling. He still feels massive and lumbering surrounded by all her things. Art supplies are expensive and he's terrified of knocking over a pot of paint which is probably worth more than all his instruments combined.

She hasn't even brought up the fact he returned pretty much empty handed the last time he went down to salvage his stuff. No clothes. They're all soaked through, including the ones he's wearing. In desperation, he'd grabbed his whisky and left everything else to fate.

"Do you want a drink?" she asks, unable to hide the annoyance in her voice.

He doesn't blame her. A few moments ago, he was trying to burst her eardrums, and now she's having to play hostess.

"Sure, we're on vacation, after all." He laughs bitterly and offers the bottle of Maker's Mark. "Feel free… if you want some."

"I'm good." She takes the bottle and heads over to the kitchen, reaching up to take a glass from the cupboard. She selects one of the rounded brandy glasses, but he bites his tongue. "Ice?"

"Yeah, please. If you have any."

She checks the freezer and throws in two cubes and then pours a generous measure of whisky over them. Maybe a little too generous.

As he reaches out to take the drink from her, his fingertip grazes against hers. It's a fleeting touch, but almost enough to make him fumble the glass. Something tightens at the pit of his stomach, and his next breath escapes him broken. "Thanks."

She withdraws her hand as though his fingers are barbed and puts both her hands behind her back. "What do we do?"

"Wait for the water to subside and then see if the road's clear, I guess."

"How long will that take?"

"Maybe tomorrow? Hopefully no longer. If we're lucky."

She cocks her head to the side and looks at him, with an accusatory scowl. "You're so calm."

He's not. He doesn't feel calm, but he won't tell her that. "We'll be okay," he says, and hopes it isn't a lie.

Her eyes rake over him, on his wet clothing which clings tight to his burly frame. "Don't you want to get changed?"

"Ah." He shifts uncomfortably. There's no easy way around this. "All my clothes got wet. I was so caught up saving the drums and stuff."

She raises her eyebrows briefly. "Priorities."

"Yeah." He laughs a little. "I mean, the drums alone cost, like… seven thousand, even without all the modifications and customizations, not to mention the extra…" He stops. She doesn't care.

"Seven thousand!" Her eyes widen. "You know you can get drums for like fifty bucks online, right?"

He can't help but chuckle. "Yeah, but you may as well be smacking a margarine tub with a pencil in that case."

"Even cheaper." She holds out her hands, as though giving him the idea to keep. Her eyebrows crease a little. "You make all that money from playing music?"

"Oh." Red heat flashes across his cheeks. "No. I wish. I teach music classes too. Like a tutor… kind of. Well, no not kind of. I am a tutor."

"Cool."

"So, if you ever want to take lessons, I'm your man." He cringes at his weak sales pitch. Is he…*flirting*? Not by normal human standards, obviously, but he's not usually this dorky. For a moment he wishes more than anything the flood water had washed him off the mountain.

"I'll keep that in mind," she smiles. "But the clothes thing is an issue. I don't think I have anything that would fit you."

Of course she doesn't. He almost laughs at the absurdity of it, at the sweetness of her suggestion. "Shame. I'd look cute in those pajama shorts."

She presses her lips together as she turns a shade darker. "Yeah, probably."

The air grows heavy between them as she stands there, backed against the kitchen counter, her knuckles bone white as she grips the edge of the sink. At last she turns, grabs a glass from the cupboard, and pours herself a double shot of whisky, grimacing as she takes the first sip. The betrayal in her eyes as she glares at the golden liquid is the look of someone who's soul just died a little.

"Look," she says, setting her glass back on the counter. She sinks her teeth into her lower lip, sending flutters through his stomach. "I'm sorry, about before…"

***

She can't help but notice the way Finn's biceps flex as he scrapes his fingers back through his hair, pushing it off his face. He pauses for a moment with his hands resting on the back of his head. "Yeah, me too. We were both kind of jerks. I'm sorry."

She almost pounces on him there and then. The sweetest smile pulls at his lips, different from the smug little grin he was flashing at her before. That was the musician, the show-man. This is Finn.

"Your drums actually do sound good. I was just…"

"They're loud," he shrugs. "I get it."

"Yeah, but you've got good rhythm." Is that even the right thing to say? Her heart thrums, louder than any drum. The corner of his mouth picks up again a little. She'll take it. "There are towels in the bathroom if you want to get out of your wet clothes. I could hang them somewhere and hope-fully they'll be dry enough to sleep in by tonight. If you need to you can sleep here…you know, on the couch."

"Sounds like a plan." He nods his head once before heading into the bathroom as though he's lived there all his life.

Beth downs the whisky, coughing as the fiery liquid scorches the back of her throat. She takes one of the old sheets she uses to cover the floor while painting, and spreads it out. Carefully, she transfers instruments onto the sheet, giving them a wipe off with a dry dish towel and hoping—even though only minutes ago she was contemplating launching them down the mountainside—they're salvageable.

"Seven thousand dollars," she whispers, in disbelief.

She handles them cautiously, as though they might shatter in her hands. Sure, he was hurtling up the stairs with them through a torrential downpour, but it would be just her luck to cause irreparable damage to them now.

She's so engrossed in the task, she doesn't notice him until he's standing right in front of her, wrapped in a fluffy white towel, which sits low at his hips. His top half is completely bare, and the sight of him sends heat flooding though her body. Those tattoos on his arms snake from wrist to shoulder, like black ink sleeves. He clutches his soggy clothes in a bundle in his hands.

His chest and soft, rounded stomach are dusted with dark, fuzzy hair. There's just so much of him. She decides then and there that if he ever hugged her, she would never be able to let go.

"Everything okay?" He asks, seemingly completely at ease being around her in nothing but a towel.

"Yeah… I thought it would be better with something to absorb the water."

"You're probably right." He balances the clothes in one hand and lazily scratches at his chest with the other, pulling her eyes back toward him. "Shit, I hope they're okay."

"Me too."

He laughs, "Liar."

As she stands, her legs are trembling. She tries very hard

not to look at him, and fails pretty much instantly. But he isn't looking at her.

He's staring at the easel, at the rough sketch of him she has copied onto canvas and begun to paint while he was drumming loud enough to wake the dead.

A wide smile spreads across his face. "Is that me?"

"Oh…" Shit. The horns. The tusks. The vivid splashes of color bursting from his drums as he hits them; midnight blue, blood red, abyssal black. Cold fear washes over her. "God, I'm so sorry. I didn't think you'd ever see it."

"It's fucking badass, Beth." Her heart skips as he strides over to it, the grin never leaving his face as he takes a closer look. "Holy crap, this is awesome."

She's burning up. His praise, along with the sight of his broad back, the muscles in his shoulders flexing as he stoops to look at her work, is enough to sway her from cautious perving to downright thirst. "Thanks."

"I'm serious. Can I buy it?"

Buy? She could really use the money, but… "No. You can have it. As an apology for me being so moody."

He shakes his head, rummages through the bundle in his arms, until he finds his wallet. He opens the brown leather bifold, pulls out a wad of notes, and starts flicking through them. "How much do you normally charge for commissions?"

"I… no, no it's free. It's an apology."

"And this is my apology for playing so loud and invading your space."

"I still need to finish it."

"Alright." He turns to her and smiles. "Tonight?"

"I was going to, but," she gestures toward him, then darts her eyes away.

"Don't let me stop you. I'll serenade you, while you paint."

She arches an eyebrow, hoping he can't tell how much she's melting inside. "On the drums?"

The quiet chuckle he gives warms her heart. That damned smile will be the death of her.

"No," he says. "Not drums."

EIGHT

S*mooth bastard.*

He's kind of proud of himself as he picks out a melody on his acoustic guitar. It's no masterpiece, but it sounds pretty enough.

Beth paints for him. She paints *him*. When she concentrates really hard, she gets an intense crease between her eyebrows, and he can't help but notice her lips part a little each time she glances at him. He doesn't dare hope she wants him as much as he wants her, and there's no way in hell he's going to make her uncomfortable when they're trapped up a mountain together. He'd rather let her slip through his fingers than make her feel like she has to escape from his grasp.

But he aches for her. Burns for her.

It's absurd. A couple of hours ago they were enemies, and now… now he's sitting on the couch wearing nothing but a towel, playing love songs to her and buying her art.

How long is it since someone made him feel like this?

How long since someone could wrap him around their little finger with so little effort. For all his brawn and bravado, he's helpless. She's beautiful, and soft, and she smells like shampoo and paint. She's a sweet, stubborn queen, and he'll gladly be her throne.

Concentrate.

He forces himself to breathe deeply, swallowing as his throat dries out. There's every possibility she has a boyfriend, or a husband even. He knows nothing about her.

But there's harmony between them, and they both become creative in each other's presence. She continues to paint while he plays. Their tiny corner of the vast, impossible universe is an unlikely oasis of peace in the storm.

When afternoon rolls by and she's showing no signs of stopping her painting, he goes downstairs, wading through half a foot of water to his refrigerator, and takes out whatever food he can salvage. He takes the supplies up to her kitchen and puts together a couple of sandwiches for them, using her loaf of sourdough. She loves pickles, he learns, and hot sauce —almost as much as he does. They eat together, watching the rain pour from the roof onto the balcony.

It's easy to forget the disaster scene below, to pretend their little sanctuary is the entire world. Beth sits at the corner of the couch, legs crossed beneath her as she balances the plate between her thighs.

"Can I see it yet?" He asks between mouthfuls.

She shakes her head and casts him a mischievous smile. "Nope."

Their eyes linger on each other, and his face heats beneath her gaze. He's the first to break eye contact.

When they're done eating, he goes back to plucking his

guitar. By the time the world beyond their haven is growing dark, he's crafting new melodies, and some of them are definitely worth remembering. He pauses to jot them down on a page of blank sheet music. When he looks up, she's staring at him, her brush loose in her grip.

"You can read music?"

Her voice catches him off guard. He'd almost forgotten her deep, silky tone. "Yeah."

"You're very talented."

His chest swells a little. Nearly everyone he knows can read music, but he'll take the compliment. "Takes one to know one."

"You might not say that when you see the painting."

He laughs quietly. He's weirdly flattered she thinks of him as being this big, hulking beast, horns and all. "Is it time?"

She sucks in her bottom lip to hide her grin, and sends a bolt of electricity through his veins. Slowly, she inches the easel round, and reveals his portrait.

"Holy fuck," he breathes, leaning forward on the couch until he's perching on the edge of the cushion. His hand clamps over his mouth. No one has ever painted him before. Hell, has anyone even looked at him this way? He looks powerful, savage, badass, like some horned god of music and chaos.

"Is it okay?" she asks.

"Okay? Beth…" He stands, nearly forgetting the towel wrapped precariously around his hips. "You're incredible."

Sparks flow through his veins as she looks up at him, and the urge to kiss her becomes unbearable.

He likes it.

She's pretty sure she's glowing as he stares wide-eyed at the painting. Her fingers reach out reflexively, longing to touch him, to brush back the tousled wave of his hair, to feel the fluff covering his soft, heavy torso.

"Beth Barlow…" he laughs a little as he reads her signature. "You have a superhero name."

He makes her smile.

She came to the mountain for silence, but perhaps what she needed was something to shake her up. Perhaps she needed to find him. Her body certainly thinks so, and her heart is quickly catching up to the idea.

The flutters in her stomach only grow more intense as he stands beside her, examining the painting, raising his big hands to touch it before realizing the paint is still wet. The warmth of his body pulses against her, carrying the scent of him; pine soap and the sharp scent of outdoors. The scent of the rain.

His shoulder is close, so close she would only have to lean forward a little to press her lips against it.

He shifts his head, ever so slightly toward her, and her breath hitches in her chest. He knows. Somehow, he knows she wants him. Heart hammering, she steps away.

"You still haven't told me how much." His voice is thick, husky. He walks over to the table and takes a sip of his whisky.

"I can't take any money from you. It was meant to be for an exhibition, for charity. We're trying to raise money for a community art center. It feels… I don't know, it feels wrong making money from it."

He nods slowly. "Alright, well if it's for charity, double it."

Crap. It would be easy to fall in love with him.

NINE

Relief washes over him as she finally accepts the cash, and tucks it safely in her backpack. Although it pains him a little, to see the money go. He had been saving to soundproof his practice room, but his neighbors are just going to have to put up with him a while longer. He's not about to let the masterpiece out of his sight.

"I'll donate it as soon as I get back," she tells him.

He just about dies when she bends down to set her bag on the floor. Though he quickly tears his eyes away from the sight of her round ass thrust up toward him, his cock still twitches. He imagines dropping to his knees behind her and burying his face in her pussy.

Turning back to the painting, he tries to distract himself with the riot of color before him. "I can't wait to show this to the rest of the band. They'll be so jealous."

As she heads over to the kitchen to clean her brushes, she flashes him a smile which nearly sends his blood boiling. "Well if they want portraits too, send them my way. I take commissions."

"Alright, but you can't make theirs as cool as mine. Deal?"

"I can't take all the credit. You're an excellent model."

Part of him thinks she might be interested in him, but a voice in the back of his mind tells him he's delusional. They barely know anything about each other beyond first names.

She cocks her eyebrow as she heads back to the couch. "Vixen's Wail, right?"

Hearing his band's name on her lips again takes him a moment to process. "Yeah… how do you know?"

"A friend of mine looked you up."

That's a good sign… maybe. It has to be, right? If she's been talking about him to her friend, it means she's been thinking about him. He's worth digging up information on. Then again, it's entirely possible and extremely understandable that she's been bad-mouthing him.

She sits on the sofa, picking blue paint from beneath her nails.

"So," he hovers between the easel and the sofa, afraid to sit beside her. He has no qualms about his body, and has never been shy, but in her presence he's all too aware of his bare skin. "What else did your spy network uncover?"

Her eyes dart to him as her lips quirk. "That you're the drummer in a symphonic metal band."

"Damn… my secret's out."

"And that's about it. She's honestly not a very good spy."

"Considering she only had my first name to go off, that's pretty impressive. And it's still more than I know about you."

She reclines, resting her arms on the back of the sofa, her shirt stretching tight over her chest. Perhaps, she sees him as completely non-threatening, and she's simply comfortable around him like his bandmates are. If that's the case, then it's cool. He's more than happy to be her friend if it's all she wants. He'd never do anything to betray her trust.

But maybe… just maybe… she's actually trying to get a rise out of him, in the most literal sense.

"Well," she says, fixing him in place with her stare. "What would you like to know?"

She can't tell if it's working. It's been so long since seduction was anything other than having some random guy grind against her ass in the bar. She can't even tell if this is seduction. Finn is completely unreadable, standing before her pretty much naked but for the towel, but entirely too cool about it. He doesn't answer her question, and perhaps he doesn't really care to know much about her.

She breathes a gentle huff of laughter and smiles at him. "Why don't you sit?"

He does, leaving one of the sofa's cushions between them. Despite the distance, he's certainly not shy about his near nudity. He drapes the arm closest to her across the back of the sofa, while he fidgets with a red guitar pick in his other hand. His thighs are parted, and straining against the confines of the towel. He has big thighs, she can tell, and she can't help but wonder if they're as hairy as the rest of him.

Heat pools at the bottom of her stomach as she imagines raking her nails along those thighs… kneeling between them…

"Every question I can think of sounds really weird." He laughs a bit. "Like I'm fishing for personal information."

"Alright, well since we're apparently now on vacation together, let's make it a game. I'll tell you two truths and a lie. You have to guess which is the lie."

He turns to her, and his face brightens. "Sure."

After a moment's hesitation she begins their game. "I'm… an artist by night, but by day I work in a call center. I recently turned thirty but I don't really remember a whole lot of my party. And…" She sinks her teeth into her lower lip. She'll keep it safe for now. Right now, she wants to get to know him better. "When I was a kid, I had a dog. A poodle named Noodle."

He laughs. "Okay. I desperately want the Noodle one to be true, and I can believe the call center one because you have a nice voice."

Her heart skips a little at the compliment. "I do?"

He nods. "I'm going to say the middle one is the lie."

"Really… do you think I'm older or younger than thirty?"

His face flushes a shade darker. "This is harassment, I refuse to answer."

A bark of laughter escapes her, and she rocks forward, placing her hand on his forearm. A jolt spreads through her body at the touch. He's so sturdy and warm. His arms are thick and muscular—presumably from drumming—and like his torso, dusted with fine, dark hair. The realization she wants nothing more than to have those arms wrapped around her, swiftly becomes a craving.

"You're wrong, I'm afraid." She chuckles. "But you'll be pleased to know that Noodle Von Doodle was very real."

He whispers, "Yes," beneath his breath and curls his fingers into a celebratory fist. "So where do you work during the day?"

"A bar," she smiles. "The Mayfly."

"Oh hey, I think I know that place!" He grins. "Just in town, right?"

"Yeah."

"So, you're pretty local?"

"Yeah pretty much, just down the mountain."

"Cool."

She must be absolutely scarlet by now. Her face prickles from the heat, from the need to climb on top of him, lose herself in all his strength and softness. "Your turn."

He sits back, and thinks for a moment. "Alright. So… I'm twenty-nine. I can play any instrument really well, but I love drums because I like being loud." He jabs at his knees with the guitar pick as he thinks. "And my grandma owns this cabin."

She stares blankly. He has her stumped. "Okay… I need to sound this one out. The instrument one is obviously true, because the evidence is right here."

He nods as a wry smile spreads across his face.

Beth side-eyes him but continues undaunted. "I spoke to the owner of the cabin when I got here. I can't decide what I imagine your grandma sounds like."

His chest shakes as he chuckles silently. "Logical. I like your approach."

"I'm going to go with the twenty-nine one being false, because it'll make me feel better about myself if you're actually older than me."

"Ahh," he grits his teeth. "I'm sorry. The instrument one was a lie."

"This game is bullshit," she pouts, throwing her head back as she opens her arms in surrender. When he stops laughing, she sits back up. "So, this is your grandma's cabin then?"

"Yep."

"That's awesome. So, you can come up here whenever you want?"

"Pretty much, as long as it isn't already booked. I still pay though. I don't want her to lose out on money just because her grandson wants to hit things for a couple of weeks."

A wide smile tugs at her lips. "That's adorable."

He shrugs. "Could you leave her a nice review, if it's not too much trouble? Someone gave her a three-star review last year because the foliage wasn't golden enough and she's still upset about it."

"I will," she promises. That bastard. She's falling so fast she's about to reach terminal velocity.

"Thanks. She'll appreciate it. And as for instruments, I'm good on guitar and keyboard, excellent on drums," he chuckles. "But the orchestral elements, the cello, violins and stuff… Mia writes those. She's our vocalist."

"And she's the one you dated?" The words leave her mouth before she can stop them.

The moments stretch on for eternity as he turns to face her, one eyebrow arched. "So your spy did find out more than just the name of the band."

"I'm sorry. I… like, it's really none of my business. It seemed rude to bring it up before."

"It's fine," he shrugs. "We did date for a little while years ago, but it felt kind of weird. Like we were just better as friends. It's all cool. We still collaborate on the song writing and obviously work together, but it's purely platonic. We're nowhere near famous but we have a fanbase, and a few of them are reluctant to let that ship sail, despite the fact she's now happily married." The air between them grows heavy as he draws a breath. "But I'm completely single. Have been for a while."

The pulse in Beth's neck is leaping and her throat is tight and dry. "Same," she all but whispers, and her eyes, her treacherous eyes, trail down to his mouth.

She moistens her own lips with the tip of her tongue and clears her throat. "Do you want to play again?"

"Yeah." Finn's heart is hammering against his ribs, and he grips the pick in his fist so she doesn't see his hands tremble. The way she looks at him makes him feel like he's burning up. "Your turn."

She pulls in a deep breath and turns her whole body to face him, drawing her knees up on the couch. The air is practically pulsing between them.

"Okay," she breathes. Her throat twitches as she swallows. "My favorite animals are penguins. I can ride a unicycle..." Another stilted breath. "And I really want to kiss you."

The world cartwheels around them. Everything else is out of focus.

There is only her.

Her eyes are wide as though she doesn't quite believe what she said. It's ludicrous, but he desperately wants her too. It was only that morning they were intent on antagonizing each other, but now... now he wants to hold her. Butterflies —no, pterodactyls—do barrel rolls in his stomach.

Please, please, don't say anything to blow this. Be cool, for once. Just kiss her.

"I..."

Don't. Man, please don't blow it.

"I kind of want them all to be true."

She laughs a little and glances sideways toward the black windows. "I'm sorry to disappoint. I can't ride a unicycle."

"Big tick for penguins though."

Just shut up!

She chuckles and looks back at him. "Yeah."

He's burning up as she inches closer, the scent of her hair flooding his senses. Her lips are so close. He could reach out, pull her to him, pin her against him and kiss her until they're both lightheaded, but he's frozen.

The room plunges into darkness

For a moment, he's pretty sure he blacks out.

The absolute silence is shattered by a forceful gust of her breath. "Are you serious?"

A blue glow shines beside him; her phone. The power must have gone out.

"Oh… shit." He laughs, relieved he isn't unconscious on the sofa. "Some timing."

The couch shifts as she stands, and the brilliant aura of her phone fades further away from him. Cupboards and drawers grind open and thud closed as she rummages through their contents. He follows her, shuffling blindly through the pitch-black living room, caught between the excitement of knowing she feels the same as he does, and the worry of what the storm will bring next.

It'll probably take the rest of his vacation to clean everything up and repair any damage the water has caused. Hopefully his grandma won't even have to know anything was wrong.

At last comes the repeated click of a lighter, and the warm glow of candlelight.

"Nothing like a little apocalypse to set the mood," she says as she lights the next candle. She gives him a slight smile as the room fills with flickering amber light. Her hands are shaking.

Taking one of the candles, he heads to the front door and opens it, peering through the darkness. He heads downstairs to check on the state of the bottom half of the cabin, shielding the candle from the biting wind. The water seems to be subsiding a little, and the rain isn't coming down so hard. "I think we'll be okay," he calls as he climbs back up the stairs. "It actually seems to be easing off a little—" His lungs empty.

She's on the couch again, a cluster of candles sitting in the center of the coffee table, her eyes dark, and fixed on him. And though he convinces himself it's a trick of the light, a mirage caused by his wildest hopes and rushing adrenaline, no matter how many times he blinks, the picture doesn't change. She slowly, deliberately, unbuttons her shirt, and peels it back to reveal her black, silky bra. Her body is curvy, and soft, and he desperately wants to touch her.

She shrugs a shoulder and laughs a little. "I was beginning to feel overdressed."

He can't speak. The sight of her, soft and sumptuous and wanting him, renders him silent. *Him.* Finn likes to make noise. He has to be heard. But right now, standing before her, he may as well be a statue.

Doubt flashes across her face as she stands. "Have I totally misread this situation?"

"No." His hoarse voice is detached from his brain. He clears his throat and tries again. "God, no."

"Good." She smiles.

He takes a step toward her. His pulse drowns out everything. She raises her face to look at him and for a moment she looks victorious.

A shiver travels through his body as she reaches up and combs back his hair.

TEN

The hunger in his eyes melts her. He leans into her touch, bowing his head a little, bringing those beautiful lips closer to her. The way he yields to her, putting her fully in control, makes her feel like an enchantress. This big, burly man quivers as she touches him.

"Is this okay?" she asks, hoping she isn't misreading anxiety as excitement.

He simply nods. His lips part as he looks at her, and her heart leaps at the pressure of his hand on her hip, his thumb brushing against the waistband of her jeans. His touch is so feathery, so tentative, it tickles, and it takes all her self-control not to wriggle from him.

The space between them closes, and at last she presses her bare skin to his. It takes her breath away; his vast, strong body held against her. He's gentle, keeping himself in check as he trails his hands around the curve of her hips, urging her closer.

Her hands skim across his torso, following the curve of his belly, up to the swell of his chest. She can't decide which part of him she wants to touch most. All of him. She wants all of him.

She reaches up, tangles her fingers in his hair and pulls him to her, pausing to savor the sensation of his lips parted so close to hers.

His breath blows warm against her mouth.

The hesitation is delicious agony, but she can't hold off any more. She rises on her tiptoes to meet him, sinking through the softness of his beard and into the warmth and gentleness of his lips. His kiss is slow, hesitant, his lips edging over hers, as though he's afraid to let go completely.

Her arms drop to his shoulders as she slides her tongue between his lips, and his groan resonates through her chest. He stumbles back, pulling her with him as he lowers himself onto the couch, and she's practically giddy as she straddles those thick thighs, the folds of the towel rumpling beneath her.

His hands are in her hair, tangled possessively as though he knows perfectly well she's smitten. He could ask anything of her and she'd do it.

It's only when his hands drop lower, fumbling with the clasp of her bra that he stops kissing her, and his breathless voice growls through the flickering light.

His eyes widen. "Sorry. I got carried away."

"Don't be." She presses closer to him, kissing a trail down his neck. "I want you."

"Are you sure?"

She nods. "I've thought about it since the first moment I saw you. I touched myself thinking of you this morning."

Something switches in him, a shift in gear which snatches the breath from her lungs, propelling them headlong into each other. Finn kisses like he drums: hard, relentless, savage.

His teeth sink into her bottom lip, and his fingers dig into her back with a ferocity which is both painful and oh-so-fucking-good.

The peace they found in each other's company shatters, making way for their passion. He lifts her onto her feet, tugging down her jeans as he kisses her stomach, the bristles of his beard brushing against her as she runs her fingers through his hair.

She laughs a little at the absurdity of it, at the time they wasted hating each other, when this is far, far more satisfying. Reaching behind her, she unhooks her bra and pulls it away. Even before it lands on the ground his lips are around her nipple, his hands grasping, palming the softness of her breasts.

"I want to taste you." His voice is thick and dark with desire.

Beth can only nod as her throat clenches. She wants him, desperately.

"Lie down," he whispers, his eyes fixed on her breasts as his breath shudders. "On your stomach."

She doesn't question him. The anticipation of what he has in mind sends her heart racing as she lies on the couch in her underwear. Time without his touch stretches on forever. She's cold without him, craving him, skin tingling with the need to feel him again.

At last, he caves to her unspoken need. He caresses her back in broad strokes, his big hands warm and rough against her smooth skin. She moans as his lips follow, kissing a trail along her spine, soft and hot, lingering, working his way up to her shoulders. And when he pushes her hair to the side and grazes his teeth against the back of her neck, it awakens something inside her; a desire to supplicate, to be dominated.

The soft curve of his belly presses against the small of her back, and he rests his weight on one arm, wrapping it around the front of her shoulders, cupping her chin in his hand as his thumb teases her lips.

Her body tingles as he bites the nape of her neck, desire pooling between her thighs. His thumb follows the curve of her lower lip, and the urge to pull it into her mouth overwhelms her. She closes her eyes, sucking on his thumb, her tongue stroking its length, as his other hand inches lower, down her back, over the curve of her ass. He groans as his fingers slide across the slickened skin of her upper thighs.

"You're so wet," he growls against the back of her neck.

She can feel it, wet and aching. She arches her back, lifting her ass toward him, parting her thighs even more, silently begging for him to touch her as her tongue caresses his thumb.

H e's rock-hard, his dick pressing against her curvy thigh, and so turned on he's lightheaded. If she touches him, he's sure he'll come instantly.

The candlelight, the wind and rain battering the cabin, the gorgeous woman writhing beneath him, pressing her hot, wet little pussy against him. It's hot as fuck, and he's going to make sure she has a good time. The way she sucks his thumb sends sparks of pleasure shooting right to his cock, and he'd love to fuck her mouth, but not tonight.

Tonight is about her.

"Do you want me to touch you?" He whispers against her ear. There's a darkness in his voice he's never heard before. Being trapped with her in the remote cabin awakens something in him. He's never been one for one-night stands, never rushed into getting physical before, but then again, he's never met anyone who turns him on as much as she does.

She nods, lifting her hips a little more. He desperately wants to move her panties to the side and touch her, but he'll take his time, drawing out her pleasure.

With the lightest touch of his fingertips, he brushes his hand against her. Her underwear is soaked and warm, the scent of her arousal flooding his senses, begging him to fuck her. Her moan vibrates against his thumb.

"Like that?"

She pulls his thumb from her mouth and gasps. "More. Please."

He obliges, stroking her slowly. Her whimper makes his cock twitch, her sharp breath tells him he's touching her how she likes it, but he knows for sure that soon it won't be enough. He wants to make this last.

"I want you," she breathes. "Please."

"Please what?" As if he doesn't know.

"Fuck me."

"Not yet," he growls. He sinks his teeth into her neck again, pinning her beneath him.

She sucks in a breath. "Is this payback?"

It's as much torture for him as it is for her. His towel has fallen away, and his cock is engorged, dark pink and ridged with thick veins, beads of pre-cum glistening from its head.

"Not at all," he whispers, slipping his hand beneath her underwear, gliding across the soft curve of her ass until he reaches the heat of her needy pussy. He hesitates before touching her, feeling her warmth pulse against his fingers.

She cries out and wriggles, desperate for his touch. "God, you're so annoying."

"And you're demanding." He withdraws his hand, as much as it pains him.

She growls beneath him, her fingers digging into the couch cushions. "I'll be good. Just… please."

He can't help but grin as he raises himself onto his hands, lifting his weight off her entirely. Her back is arched, her ass high in the air, the tops of her thighs gleaming. He wishes he was the artist, because he'd paint this; her lying exactly as she is, bathed in candlelight, begging for his touch, wet and wanting him. She's the most beautiful thing he has ever seen.

"You have to promise to be good to me from now on." He sits behind her, brushing his fingers against her panties one last time, drawing a desperate cry from her.

"I will," she whispers. "I promise."

He leans forward, grazing his teeth against her ass cheek. "I can practice whenever I want, make as much noise as I want?"

"Yes."

"And while I drum, you'll lie on the couch, or on the bed, playing with yourself until I'm done and then I'll fuck you while I'm hot and sweating."

"Oh, fuck yes."

He grins and kisses her through her underwear. The scent of her is fucking intoxicating. It's more than he can bear. Slowly, he pulls down her panties. She's hot, and wet, and just inches from his lips. Her breath is ragged, and she leans back toward him, silently begging him for release. Her clit is swollen, half-hooded and glistening, but she'll have to wait a little longer. Watching her squirm is too delicious.

ELEVEN

S he could kill him.

His breath blows hot against her, and she just knows he has that smug little grin on his face. But she has to play nice. There are rules to this game, unspoken, but mutually understood. She is his tonight. The bite marks at the back of her neck are a claim, and now she has to play by his rules.

It suits her fine. Next time, she'll get her own way. Next time she'll sit on his smug, irritatingly handsome face and ride his smart mouth until she can barely walk.

That fucker.

"Tell me what you want." His voice is so deep, thick and gravelly. He's every bit as turned on as she is, but he's drawing it out, torturing the both of them.

"I want you to lick me," she says. "And then I want your cock."

He makes a low humming sound, his breath barely whispering against her. "Do you have a condom?"

"In my bag. I have an implant too."

"Good." There's a heavy silence and then, "Look how hard you make me, Beth."

She turns around to look at him, and the sight hardens her lungs. His towel has gone, and he's completely naked, sitting behind her, his cock hard against his belly. Everything about him is big, powerful. Hers.

"So, the drum kit isn't compensation at all?"

He laughs a little, and there's a trace of that sweet smile. "More like a counterweight."

Smug and so fucking irresistible.

He draws closer, and her heart hammers as he touches her again. He parts her folds, exposing her completely. She's almost sobbing as he touches her with the very tip of his fingers. So good, but not enough. "Finn, please. I want you so much. Please."

Nothing can prepare her for the sensation of his tongue sliding against her, sliding into her. Her toes curl as she pushes back against him, desperately trying to angle herself so he can lick her clit, but no matter how she moves, he doesn't. He's doing it on purpose.

"Oh, fuck, Finn."

He's insatiable, savoring every second. It's exquisite, and frustrating, delicious and agonizing. She reaches between her legs, stroking her clit to find release, but he takes her hand and pins it to the couch, denying her.

"Cruel," she whimpers.

"The cruelest." She can *hear* his grin. He knows she loves it. "I'll tease you all night if you don't behave."

She gasps as he pushes two fingers into her, stroking her, and slowly thrusting. When he withdraws them, she turns again to meet his dark eyes.

"Taste yourself," he orders.

Heat fans over her as she takes his fingers into her mouth, coating her tongue with her own slickness, slightly salty and faintly sweet all at once. His eyes never falter from watching her as his lips part, and a broken breath signals his own agony.

"Fuck." His throat flexes as he swallows.

"I'll do anything you ask," she says. It's a power trip, knowing the effect she has on him. "Just make me come."

He nods, lazily stroking her labia with his thumb. "Then I want you to come to my show." He whispers. "I want to see you again."

She closes her eyes, drawing a deep breath as he stokes her pleasure. "I'll come to your show, I'll watch you drum, and I'll touch myself the whole time."

He groans.

"You'll be stuck on the stage, knowing I'm coming while I'm thinking about you. Knowing I'm touching my pussy and wishing it was your hand." Her breath catches as he grasps her hips and flips her over, his rough hands sliding round to cup her ass as he pulls her toward him, hooking her legs over his broad shoulders.

She can barely breathe. The anticipation is overwhelming as his lips stop so close to her clit, she can almost, *almost* feel them.

But he turns his head, kissing her inner thighs as his lips curve into a smile. "Then I'll come to your exhibition," he whispers. "And we'll find somewhere secret where I can hide you away and lick this beautiful pussy."

"Yes. God, yes."

At last, he bows his head and kisses her clit, his tongue caressing her with long languid strokes. She resists the urge to close her eyes, and watches him, transfixed at the pink flash of his tongue, and his lips, caress her swollen skin, harder, faster. He raises his eyes to look at her, and his approving groan tips her over the edge. He keeps licking her as she comes, as she tangles her hands in his hair, holding her to him as though if he pulled away, she would die. She might.

When she comes back down to earth, he positions himself between her thighs, laces his fingers with hers, and holds her hands above her head. She can taste herself on his lips as he tenderly kisses her.

"Are you okay?" he whispers between kisses.

"Very."

He chuckles as she looks up at him with heavy half-lidded eyes. "You're so gorgeous, Beth."

Raising her head to kiss him again, a shiver courses through her body as her nipples brush against his chest hair. He doesn't enter her, not yet, even as his cock strains hard between their bodies.

The promises they made to each other in the heat of passion echo through her mind. She has every intention of keeping them.

Finn's mind is racing. He's never been one to rush things, never indulged in casual sex. But this doesn't feel casual. He trusts her. Hell, if he isn't careful, he'll blurt out that he loves her.

There's such intensity between them. She's magnetic, addictive, and he feels safe with her. The taste and scent of her arousal covers him, and despite him being in charge so far, she's the one who has completely claimed him.

He can't take his eyes from her curvy, naked body as she

crosses the room, her legs still a little unsteady. Being in control of her pleasure was fun, but for whatever comes next, she's fully in command. A man his size could easily seem overpowering or intimidating, and that's the last thing he wants.

He's hers now, to do with as she pleases.

When she returns with a condom, his cock twitches in some Pavlovian response. She kneels between his thighs and strokes his length slowly. Her touch is soft, far softer than he ever touches himself. Compared to his rough hands, hers are silk. It's all he can do to remind himself to keep breathing.

She watches him, gauging his reaction, humming in approval as he tosses his head back, unable to keep his cool a moment longer. Her hands slide through beads of pre-cum as he grips the edges of the couch cushions.

His breath hitches as she unwraps the condom and rolls it onto his cock. She looks up at him with those big, intoxicating eyes. "How do you want me?"

"I'm all yours," he says, his voice rough. Heat spreads across his chest. "You're in charge now."

A smile tugs at her lips. "That's brave, after all your teasing."

"I trust you."

She climbs onto his lap, straddling his thighs as her pussy brushes the head of his cock. The heat of her tightens a knot in his belly. He can only flex his fingers, gripping the cushions to stop himself from pulling her down onto him.

"Look at you," she whispers, running her hands through the hair on his chest. "So handsome. You're blushing."

"You make me feel like I'm burning up, Beth."

She takes his hand, and he can barely contain himself anymore as she guides it to her breasts. So soft and warm.

Her nipples are hard, and she presses her lips together as he swipes his thumb across them.

She lowers her hips a little, so achingly close. Her heat pulses against his cock as she begins to slowly grind her hips, teasing him. The way she moves enraptures him. It's a slow, rolling rhythm, a promise of how she'll make him feel when she's good and ready; when she decides he deserves it. She's completely in control of his pleasure and she knows it.

The muscles in his thighs clench in anticipation.

"So beautiful," he whispers. "God, I want you."

"I know," she says, just as breathless as he is.

Burning just as hot.

TWELVE

She's a goddess. The lust and hunger in his eyes tell her way before his lips.

As she sinks down onto his cock, he can't contain his moan. A thrill courses though her, tingling along her spine, tightening her nipples as he fills her.

He buries his face in her tits, licking and sucking her nipples as she rides him. His hips buck, thrusting up into her, deeper and harder, until she's gasping too. He can't get enough of her, and she can barely breathe as she rides him, overwhelmed, bodies blazing, hands grasping.

She could spend hours exploring his body, but any longer and she'll combust. "You're perfect." The words tumble out of her, carried on her broken breaths. "I could love you."

He draws a sharp breath as his teeth graze her shoulder. "Me too. God, me too Beth."

Her back arches as he slips his hand between them, sliding his fingertips against her slick, swollen clit. He rubs her hard, frantic, as though his own pleasure hinges on hers, and he won't allow himself to come until she does.

Her orgasm tears through her, rendering her motionless as she rides savage waves of pleasure.

His fingers grip her hips as he comes, thrusting deep into her, his composure collapsing as he presses his head back against the cushions and whispers her name.

They wrap their arms around each other as the intensity ebbs, and through quiet laughter they come back to earth. The rain patters on the rooftop, and it's a while before she realizes the power came back.

"Well, shit," Finn laughs, kissing the bite marks on her shoulders.

She returns his grin and runs her fingers through his hair, pushing it back from his face. "That escalated."

He looks at her as though he can't believe she's real.

Her heart is laid bare, but it feels safe in his hands.

Unexpected doesn't cover it. She nestles against his chest, her fingers tracing the patterns of the tattoos on his arms as he breathes in the scent of her hair. Somehow, they fit together perfectly, their fires consuming each other in one blazing inferno. He holds her gently, all too aware of the strength of his arms.

The lights are back on, and the rain is little more than a shower, the world around them calm and peaceful at last.

His mind races as he searches for the right thing to say, but nothing he can think of even comes close to expressing the thoughts tangled in his head. "I guess it's my turn now?"

She raises her head, her eyes scanning his features. He expects her to crack a joke, but she's silent, waiting.

"Okay," he clears his throat. "So, which is the lie?" It

seems absurd that his heart starts frantically pounding as she waits for him to speak. They're naked, holding each other, basking in the aftermath of fucking each other senseless, and he's still so afraid of rejection. "Number one: I once ran a two-minute mile but no-one believes me."

She laughs, and the warmth in her eyes melts the icy fear flowing through his veins.

"Two…" He's beaming, his heart leaping in his chest. "I meant everything I said about wanting to see you again. And three: I know we barely know each other and I hope this doesn't scare you off, but… I feel as though my life just completely changed."

The way she sinks her teeth into her lower lip sends a flutter of arousal through his stomach. He's quickly learning that when it comes to Beth, he's insatiable.

"I think so too." She kisses him, over and over, her soft, full lips drawing him in.

With every kiss she secures a little piece of his heart, and as they make their way to the bed, giddy with the loveliness and absurdity of it all, he's absolutely certain he could give it all to her.

Eyes closed and nestled against her back he breathes in her scent. "I can't wait to see you tomorrow."

Thirteen

Finn is still sleeping when daylight wakes her. The sky is bright but cloudy. Light streams in through the rain-specked windows and the small skylight above the bed.

The big, burly man surrounds her; strong arms holding her tenderly, thick legs curled against hers. His soft body pressed against her, the curve of his belly flush with her back, is warm and perfect. It's heaven. His breath is slow and steady, deep, still dreaming. Her stomach flutters as she remembers.

An alarm clock on the nightstand flashes 07:36, counting the hours and minutes since the power came back on. She could happily fall back asleep, but she really has to pee.

Finn doesn't stir as she reluctantly slips away from him. Her toes curl as they touch the cold floorboards, and as she looks back, her heart already aches with the need to climb back into bed with him, to feel safe and warm in his arms.

She hurries to the bathroom, tiptoeing so she doesn't wake him.

On the way back, the flashing green light on the top of

her cell phone catches her eye. She unlocks it to find seven missed calls from Sadie, and one text which reads: *"Something happened, didn't it? Spill!"*

The phone vibrates in Beth's hand. She rolls her eyes, biting back a laugh, and answers the call. "Hm?"

"How big was it?" Sadie all but screeches down the phone.

Beth can barely suppress her laughter as she rushes out to the balcony, closing the screen door behind her. If she doesn't wake him, perhaps she can still climb into bed with him after the call. "How do you know we did anything?"

The question doesn't detract from Sadie's excitement. "Listen, I'm living vicariously through you. Okay? Don't play coy. Tell me."

Beth smiles and braces her elbows on the balcony, looking out toward the looming mountains. An eagle circles overhead, riding the air currents. "We had a storm last night, and his floor got flooded."

"Oh my days, stop. Then what?"

"I painted him, and he bought the painting. He paid twice what I asked for because it's for charity."

"Holy shit, Beth. And then…?"

She chuckles silently pausing long enough to let Sadie squirm. "He spent the night."

"Yes!" The creak of Sadie's bed springs on the other end paints the image of her bouncing with glee. "So how was it?"

Beth's stomach flutters. "Incredible."

A choked squeal crackles from Sadie's end. "Get his number. Keep him. Never let him go, okay. You have to tell me everything when I pick you up this afternoon, okay? I need details."

"Okay."

"Beth, shit, are you in love now? I can hear it in your voice."

Something shutters inside Beth. It would be so easy to love Finn, to spend every day in those arms, but it's reckless, and she knows it. The intensity between them makes no sense, and she'll never hear the end of it if she admits she caught a bad case of feelings after sleeping with him once. "It was just one night." Her heart sinks a little as she says it aloud. It feels like a betrayal. "I doubt I'll ever even see him again."

"Ugh, that's no fun. Maybe things will work out. You never know."

Beth makes a quiet, non-committal humming sound.

Sadie sighs on the other end. "How bad was the storm?"

Lowering her eyes, Beth grimaces at the mud and debris washed up on the road. If she didn't have work that evening, she'd offer to stay and help Finn try to fix the mess. Hell, she'd gladly stay forever. "It was pretty bad."

"Damn, I'm glad you're okay," Sadie says "I can't believe he paid double for your painting. You must feel like—"

"An absolute asshole."

Sadie laughs. "Oh no, you complained about him so many times."

"I know. It was super shitty. I honestly hate myself for it."

"Yeesh." Sadie grows silent as the tinkling sound of cat kibble tumbling into a ceramic dish echoes down the receiver. Beth smiles, holding back on the oft-repeated joke of Sadie's neighborhood having the fattest strays in the country. At last, Sadie comes back to the phone. "Go and enjoy your last few hours with him. For fuck's sake get his number. I'll be there in a few hours to pick you up, okay. I'll let you know if I have any trouble getting there."

"Thank you." Her heart leaps with the excitement of a few more hours with Finn. She's giddy with the notion of climbing back into bed, waking him with kisses, and exploring his beautiful body. "I'll see you later."

"Laters."

She turns, and heads back inside.

FOURTEEN

He's alone when he wakes, afraid he's dreamt the whole thing.

Because it had to be a dream. There was no way on this earth any of it could've happened, but the scent of her lingers on his body, and he's in her bed, isn't he?

His heart leaps at the muffled sound of her voice. She's real. It happened.

He climbs out of bed and ventures out of the bedroom, cock still semi-hard, to find her standing on the balcony in nothing but a t-shirt and panties. Her phone is pressed to her ear, one foot sliding up and down the opposite calf. God, she makes his heart glow.

Desire overcomes him, the desire to walk out there, wrap his arms around her, maybe even to fuck her right there out in the open. He steps forward, and her voice becomes clearer.

"It was just one night. I doubt I'll ever see him again."

It hurts a little to hear it, but he likes her. He wants to make it work. Perhaps like him, she's cautiously optimistic.

"It was pretty bad. An absolute asshole… It was super shitty. I honestly hate myself for it."

His blood runs cold.

With every word she utters, his heart, which he had lain before her so open and bare, closes and hardens. He's always fallen too hard, too fast. Her words leave him wounded.

Heat scorches his face. She *hates* herself. Hates herself for touching him, for fucking him. There's no talking this through. He doesn't need a performance review, or a critique of his rusty techniques. No, he needs to get the hell out of there and preserve what little dignity he still has.

He hurries back to the room and throws on his damp clothes, unable to bear the shame of her seeing him nude, still hard for a woman who thinks so little of him. There's an ache in his chest which won't leave; anger, confusion and pain. He walks back out to the living room and sits on the couch, replaying what happened, feeling as though pieces of him are flaking and drifting away.

It has to be some kind of mistake. It has to be.

His breath hitches as she ends the call. And the second before she slides open the glass doors lasts forever.

Any doubt he had of her disgust in him vanishes as she steps inside and her eyes meet his. Her disappointment is unbearable, and the wounds she's already clawed open begin to fester.

Like any other injured animal, he doubles down on his defense. He stands up and backs away from her. "Hey, so, thanks for last night. I'm gonna head downstairs and try and make headway on the damage."

"Oh…" She frowns a little and folds her arms over her chest. "Yeah, no problem. It looks like there's a lot to do."

"Yeah."

"Want any help cleaning up?"

"I've got it. Thanks." He takes a step toward the door, and the proud voice in the back of his mind admonishes him for letting it end on her terms. He has to say something, has to show her how little her rejection affects him. "Look, I'm leaving for the tour in a couple of weeks… this would never have worked anyway, but it was fun, I guess."

Her face hardens. "Oh."

And that's it. That's all she can say.

The humiliation of picking up the portrait is too much. Last night, the snarling, powerful beast was a compliment, but now… now it hurts. In her eyes he's lumbering, hideous, and she hates herself for touching him. *Hates* herself.

He leaves without another word. The door clicks behind him, and his boots pound the stairs. Lumbering. Hideous. The part of his mind which had him convinced she could love him retreats.

When he reaches the bottom of the stairs and he's faced with the full extent of the damage, his eyes begin to sting. The thick mud coating the floorboards, staining the bottom few inches of upholstery on the couch, blurs as he blinks back tears. His bed is sodden, and with a heavy heart he realizes he'll have to spend the next week or so sleeping in the upstairs bed anyway. Alone.

No doubt she'll tell her friends what a terrible lay he was, and they'll all have a good laugh. It'll probably be all over Vixen Wail's social media pages by tomorrow.

"Fuck this." He slams the door closed, and gets to work.

FIFTEEN

The afternoon sun warms Beth's back as her hand hovers mid-air in front of the lockbox. The cold, jagged edge of the key presses against her palm. A debate rages inside her; whether to lock it in there and slip away silently, retaining at least a shred of her dignity, or go downstairs and confront him.

For all the noise he can make on the drum kit, Finn's somehow even louder with a sweeping brush. The sound of him moving around down there hits her like a punch to the chest. It's definitely not the first time a guy has gone cold the morning after, but it still stings. She liked him. She really did. He didn't seem the type to fuck and duck, but she reminds herself over and over, she never really knew him.

The version of Finn she held in her arms last night was easy to love, but the man crashing around down there… he's brash and boorish and just downright rude. She vows to keep her cool next time, to keep her heart locked away until she's certain, and then maybe a little bit longer.

Still, a masochistic part of her wants to see him one more

time. She could go down and give him the key herself, since he'll have to go up there to get his instruments. He'll likely stay upstairs so he has someplace dry to sleep.

Her forehead creases. Her heart screams at her to demand to know what the fuck happened.

No.

She refuses to become a laughing stock; a desperate chick who got attached after one good fuck. He'll probably tell his bandmates she was a groupie.

Fuck him.

She locks away the key, and releases a breath. It's done. It's over.

That morning some foolish part of her had entertained the idea that perhaps there could be a future for them after all. She won't make that mistake again. Not for a while, anyway.

"You okay?" Sadie calls from the bottom of the steps, wrinkling her nose at the mud caking the bottom of her pristine white sneakers.

"Yeah," Beth lies.

She makes her way slowly down the stairs, clinging to her easel and painting supplies. He'd left the portrait she did of him behind when he bailed, but he'd paid for it, so she couldn't take it back. She had left it on the kitchen counter top, along with his whisky.

Ever the dutiful deputy, Sadie glowers at the wooden exterior wall of the bottom floor, and though she can't see him, she flips him off. "Jerk."

Beth forces a smile. She'll allow herself to mope on the car ride home, and then, as soon as she steps through her door, she'll force herself to forget him.

Shoving her supplies into the back of Sadie's jeep, she

casts one last glance at the cabin, despite her better judgement.

Movement in the bottom window catches her eye and sets her lungs like cement. The image of him is somewhat distorted and dimmed by the way the light reflects on the window. His attention is focused entirely on sweeping. His hair is unruly, and he's still wearing the same clothes as yesterday.

"You ready?" Sadie asks as she climbs into the driver's seat.

A voice in the back of Beth's head screams at her, begs her to ask him what happened. What changed? Was he lying when he said he wanted to see her again? Did it mean nothing when he told her she'd changed his life?

"Let's just get out of here," she mutters, climbing in beside Sadie. Shame scalds her cheeks.

They pull off, gravel crackling beneath the tires, as the trees consume the cabin. It doesn't take long before the gravel runs out, and the road's uneven surface jolts Beth and Sadie around.

"What the fuck happened, Beth?" Sadie asks as she battles with the road. "One minute you said it was incredible, and the next…"

Beth shakes her head, picking at the paint beneath her fingernails. "I don't know. Last night he was… it seemed like we clicked. More than clicked. But this morning, he changed. After I spoke to you, he just turned cold."

Sadie makes a choked sound of disgust at the back of her throat. The hardness in her eyes indicates that her mom-friend instincts are fully activated. "Oldest trick in the book. I'm a huge advocate for one-night stands, but you have to be safe. You need to protect yourself from STDs *and* STAs." She winces as they drive over a pothole. "That's sexually transmitted affection, by the way. Protect your parts, and your heart. He's a dick for leading you on like that."

Beth forces a smile and releases a heavy breath. "Thanks. Yeah."

"If you want, you can come to my place for dinner, and we'll leave shitty anonymous comments on his band's YouTube videos?"

"Dinner would be nice, thanks."

Sadie nods slowly as they make their way down the mountainside. Anticipation coils in Beth's gut as she awaits the next barrage of questions and advice.

She's ready for it when her friend sinks her teeth into her lower lip and suppresses a grin. "So, on the phone you said it was incredible. What exactly does 'incredible' entail?"

Beth laughs quietly and turns toward the window, as the trees pass by. He's up there, somewhere. Her scent is probably still tangled in the hair of his beard. She wonders if his skin tingles like hers does in all the places he kissed her.

***

The gravel crackles as she drives away, and focusing on the task is all Finn can do to stop himself from running out after her. He was so sure she loved last night as much as he did. He knows she fell asleep in his arms, kissing him. So how the hell did it turn so sour?

She made a fool of you, man.

A voice in the back of his head tells him he's been naive. He barely knew her, but he got attached, far, far too soon. She appeared in his life like a tornado, picked him up, turned his world upside down and left him broken and bruised.

He pulls out his phone and takes a note of the tornado thing. Lyrics. At least something came out of it.

Despite working on the cabin all morning, he's made little progress on cleaning out the mud. He'll have to call someone to come up there and fix it up properly.

His phone vibrates in his hand, and for one absurd moment, he thinks it could be Beth. The word "G'ma" flashes across the screen.

He releases a sigh and swipes his thumb across the screen to answer. "Hi Gigi."

"Finn?" His Grandma's voice is faint on the other end. The signal still isn't great. "Are you okay? I was worried."

"Yep." He stares out toward the empty woods, to where the road disappears behind the trees. "Everything's okay."

"Was anything damaged in the storm?"

He swipes an arc through the mud on the floor with the toe of his sneaker. "Um. Yeah, but don't worry. I can call out the insurance people and get it all fixed up. You don't have to do a thing."

Her sigh of relief on the other end of the line is completely worth the effort and expense of the cleanup. "I was so worried."

"It's all good. Don't worry. I'm safe, and the cabin is going to be fine."

"What about the lady upstairs? Do you think she enjoyed her stay?"

Thinking of Beth is like taking a knife to the gut. Every minute he spends bailing out rainwater, and cleaning out mud, steals a little of her scent from him. Soon he'll have nothing but a memory which he can scarcely believe is true, and the twisting pain her words have left in his chest.

"She said she'd leave you a good review." He hopes, if nothing else, that wasn't a lie.

"Oh, that's wonderful. Bless her. Alright baby, I'll see you in a week, okay? You'll come to see me before you go on tour, won't you?"

"Of course. I love you."

"Love you too, bye. Be good."

She hangs up.

All at once the destruction, humiliation and loneliness crushes him, toppling onto him as though the cabin itself has collapsed, burying him beneath the rubble. He's not only heartbroken and humiliated, but humiliated at being heart-broken over someone he barely even knows.

But he'll dig his way out, out of the rubble, out of the pit he slipped into when he fell for her.

Later that evening, he trudges upstairs, aching, exhausted and filthy, and punches the code into the key safe. His guts twist as he opens the door. She has cleaned, put everything back in its place, and set his things on the counter carefully. The top floor is pristine, but somehow the devastation there is so much worse.

Sixteen

"This is shit."

Beth tears out the page in her sketch pad, scrunches it, and hurls the balled-up sheet across the room.

Two weeks. Two weeks of trying and failing since she left the cabin.

No inspiration, nothing.

She storms out of the spare bedroom in her apartment she uses as a studio, traipses down the hall and flops onto her bed, burying her face in the forest-green duvet. There's only one thing on her mind, one image she can't shake no matter how hard she tries to ignore it.

With a sigh, she rolls onto her back, pulls her phone out of her pocket and calls Sadie.

Old Reliable picks up after three rings. "What's happening, baby girl?"

"I'm broken. I can't paint. Well, I can, but the only thing I *want* to paint is the thing I'm not supposed to be thinking of."

"You're not broken. You're being haunted, that's all."

Beth frowns and rolls back onto her stomach. "Am not."

Sadie chuckles on the other end of the line. "Are too. Haunted by the memory of that beard rasping against your thighs."

Her stomach flips at the thought, but she makes herself scowl. "Stop."

A long pause and then. "Did you call me for permission?"

"No!" Beth stands and walks back to her studio. "Maybe?"

"Paint him then. Get it out of your system. You may as well get something out of it."

"Thanks. Yeah. You're right."

She ends the call, and gets to work. Once she starts, it's impossible to stop. She works straight onto the canvas, creating the piece she's been holding back on ever since she left the cabin; her and Finn, an explosion of light and fire and color, bodies entwined, backs arched in ecstasy. She obscures his face with grasping fingers, splayed across his cheek and jaw. It's beautiful, intimate, and frankly, sexy as hell. Gold and copper shimmer in his beard, and she takes painstaking care over every detail of him; his tattoos, the shape of his body, everything she has committed to memory.

When evening draws in, and she's too tired and hungry to go on, she sits with a bowl of vegetable soup and a sourdough roll, her laptop perched on the arm of the sofa.

Her fingers flex with the need to look him up, but she won't. She can't. It's bad enough she's painting him. Bad enough she spent three goddamn hours making sure she painted his tattoos just right. She can't.

She won't.

She releases a breath and stares defeated as the Vixen's

Wail homepage loads, and he glowers at her from the thumbnails of the recommended videos. The words 'watch again?' glare at her like an accusation.

Tomorrow she'll work on something different, push him out of her head and focus on something else. She'll accept it for what it was; a one-night-stand with a guy who played her like a fucking maestro. Tomorrow.

***

"Fucking hell, Finn."

He waits, his breath a solid mass in his lungs as Mia pores over the lyrics. The band's vocalist blinks slowly, her brow creased, either in concern or confusion. She fusses with the midnight blue tip of one of her braids, poking it against her cheek.

The purple light in the back of the RV casts violet highlights on her dark brown skin, and the crimson contact lenses she's experimenting with give her a kickass vampiric look. The fans are going to dig it.

For all Finn's talent, Mia is the powerhouse of Vixen's Wail. Her voice, and the way she uses it to craft emotion in their music, is nothing short of incredible. Having her look over his attempt at putting his raw feelings into lyrics is absolutely terrifying, no matter how long they've been friends.

The band has been on the road for a month, travelling in a rented RV from venue to venue. So far, the tour is amazing, and he's even managed to go a few minutes without thinking of *her*. It's everything he's ever dreamed of, but he isn't content.

"Are you okay?" Mia can always see right through him. They've worked together for more than ten years, and have been through so much. She knows him, and can always see deep beneath the surface of his skin where he's rawest.

"Yeah." He nods and tries to smile.

"This woman hurt you, didn't she?"

"Alright, whose ass are we kicking?" Nic, the band's violinist chips in from the back of the RV, hidden behind a cluster of cardboard merch boxes. They stand and pound their bone-white fist into the center of their palm. "Vixens assemble."

Finn chuckles and shakes his head. "I'm alright, honestly. No ass-kicking required."

Nic pouts and slumps back down into the seat, tossing their long, bleached white hair over their shoulder. "Got my knuckles all excited for nothing."

"I can definitely work with these lyrics," Mia smiles, turning Finn's attention back to her. "And seriously, if you need to talk about anything…"

Finn shrugs a shoulder dismissively, and glances out of the window, at the endless streets of crowded chain stores rolling by. In a couple more nights, the tour will be over, and they'll get to play their triumphant hometown show. It's the biggest venue they've played, and it's close to being their first sell-out show.

"I'm good." He nearly convinces himself.

Mia's eyes bore into him though, and he can almost hear the reprimand trapped behind her smile. "So, what's this song called?" She asks finally.

"I was thinking *B.B.*"

"As in, the letter B?"

"Yeah. Twice."

She raises her eyebrows. "Well, it's no worse than your last title suggestion."

"Hey now," Finn laughs. "*Cacoffiny* is a masterpiece!"

"Agree to disagree." Mia lets the braid fall and rests her chin on the heel of her hand, tapping her crimson talons one by one along the curve of her cheekbone. "So, B.B...?"

As Mia's eyes dart to the painting of him hanging above his bed, her grin dissipates. He scolds himself for being so obvious. Pity is the last thing he needs, because he knows himself, and he knows he'll wallow in it if given the chance.

"Beth Barlow." She reaches out and takes his hand. There was a time when that gesture would've set his blood alight, but now there's nothing but camaraderie. "You know you can talk to me Finn."

The other members of the band are either only half-listening, or fully listening and only half pretending not to be. He doesn't mind. They're family. Perhaps it would be good to get it all off his chest, to release the burning confusion and hurt from its cage behind his ribs. He draws a deep, slow breath as the lyrics sheet blurs in front of him.

"I've been a complete dipshit." It's painful to say aloud, but once he starts, it's impossible to stop.

Mia listens as he pours his heart out. Of course, he doesn't tell her all the physical details, but the emotional ones...he surprises even himself as he admits how much he let Beth mean to him.

Nic comes to sit beside Mia tearing up a receipt as they both listen, the violinist arching one perfectly preened eyebrow in disbelief. By the time Finn finishes, his cheeks are burning, and he doesn't doubt they're practically glowing neon pink. But it's out there in the open, the story of how he fell for Beth, only to find his feelings were entirely one-sided.

"Wait. You stormed out on the woman of your dreams over half a phone call?" Nic rolls their eyes. "She could've been talking about anything. The storm, her art, the fact you were drinking whisky at 9 a.m.… anything!"

The world tilts a little. Finn stares ahead, trying to grasp at the sliver of hope, only to have it slip through his fingers. "No." He shakes his head. "She said she hated herself for what she'd done. That's the part that got me. What we did made her *hate* herself. I made her hate herself."

Mia's eyes glaze over as she raises her eyebrows. "That's rough."

"I know." Finn swipes his hands back over his hair and rests them on the back of his head. "This is why I never do the casual thing. I can't stop thinking about her. It felt so right, and then… bam."

The silence in the RV is broken only by the gentle rumble of the engine, and the soft click of the blinkers as they make their way around a corner. Instinctively, the band members brace themselves, holding on to anything fastened down as they lean into the turn.

"Do you want to start working on the melody for this song?" Mia offers, sensing his need to change the subject.

He inhales sharply, and pulls a sheet of music from the folder beside him. It's the sheet he'd worked on while Beth stood in front of him, painting him. Her song, the one he tortures himself with constantly.

"I already started."

Seventeen

"Holy crap." Sadie presses her fingertips to her lips as she stares wide-eyed at the painting.

Beth stands back, her heart beating so hard against her ribcage she feels like it's about to burst out of her chest. Even face down, ass up on the couch in the cabin she didn't feel this exposed.

Sadie laughs and claps her hands together. "I honestly think this is the best you've done, although my judgement may be clouded by the fact that it's hot as Hades."

Beth cringes. "Appropriate for charity though?"

"Oh fuck no," Sadie grins. "But I guarantee it'll raise a lot of money for them."

"I don't know," Beth crosses the room and searches through her portfolios for the thousandth time, looking for something else for the exhibition. "It feels like I'm exposing us both."

"I don't think so. I only know who he is because you told me. It's abstract enough that it keeps both your identities secret, and you can't see his face fully. I think it's fine. Better than fine." She stares at it a moment longer. "If I had the money, I'd buy it."

"You want my nipples on your wall?"

"Ugh, I thought you'd never ask." Sadie cackles and picks her bag up from the floor. "I feel like as your friend I should tell you I don't really approve of something so beautiful being created to honor an asshole who walked out on you after playing with your heart like he did."

Beth frowns. "You told me to paint him—"

"I didn't think it was going to be *this* good." She sucks her breath between her teeth before she puts her hand inside her purse. "Okay, so you're probably going to be super mad at me."

"I'm never mad at you." Beth leans back, perching on the edge of her desk. "What did you do?"

"I might have maybe bought tickets to Vixen's Wail's show tonight."

Heat courses through Beth's body as her jaw clenches. "Yeah, okay I'm mad at you."

Sadie cringes a little, gritting her teeth together as she pulls the tickets from her wallet and holds them between her thumb and forefinger. "We don't have to go. It was just an idea. We could stand way, way back and… I don't know. I thought seeing him again might cure you. Like, it might take some of the mystery away. Plus, I'm actually kind of into their music now. I've been listening since…You know."

Beth sighs. The painting of her and Finn, entwined in a passionate, climactic embrace looms bright in the corner of her vision. He's become a constant specter, a source of wonder. The burning question of what might have been, and what went wrong; simultaneously an asshat for leaving, and the best lover she's ever had. Schrödinger's fuckboy.

If she saw him again, perhaps… perhaps she'd see he was wrong for her all along.

As ridiculous as Sadie's plan is, it just might work.

Beth releases a labored sigh and rolls her eyes. "Can we dress up like goths?"

The squeal which erupts from Sadie has an inhuman, banshee-like quality. "Yes! Oh, dear gods yes!"

The mountain haunts Finn, a distant, hazy monument to his humiliation as he unloads the RV.

He tries not to look. Being back home, so close to the place where his heart was torn out, picks at his healing wound. Somewhere up there is the cabin; pristine, freshly painted, carpeted, and refurnished. That weekend cost him a lot, but the money can be re-saved. The other stuff… well, that might take a little longer.

He climbs down the vehicle's steps, and walks toward the pile of boxes, amplifiers and instrument cases.

"This is awesome," Nic grins as they lift their violin case. "Easily the nicest venue we've played."

"Oh, for sure." Finn shields his eyes as he looks around the loading bay. An iron fence surrounds them, keeping their equipment safe while they unload, and holding the smattering of early, diehard fans, back from following them backstage. It makes a change from unloading in the dank alleyways behind the dive bars they played in other cities.

The rest of the band lug the heavy cases of equipment into the venue, and the air crackles with excitement when they're near. The fans beyond the fence cheer whenever they spot them. Mia, and Nic, Anya the guitarist, Tamika the bassist, Liz the keyboardist, and Jordan the cellist, laugh and wave, giddy with the band's burgeoning success. Their excitement is contagious, but the effect is short-lived. The second he's left alone, shielded by the RV, all he can see is the mountain.

"You okay?" Mia asks as she returns to his side and dabs her forehead on her sleeve.

"Yeah, just… it's weird to be back, you know?"

"Do you have anyone coming tonight?"

He shakes his head and shoves his hands in his pockets, toeing the corner of one of the cardboard merch boxes. His shows are too loud for Gigi, and his mom and dad don't really *do* that kind of thing. The one and only time they came to see his high-school band play, they had an argument so explosive it almost split them entirely. Since then, for the most part they treat his music as their bad luck charm.

"You don't think she'll show up?"

Mia's question stills his heart.

"She?" He knows exactly who she means. He sniffs sharply and shakes his head, turning his back on the fence. "No. She's probably done everything she can to forget about me."

Back in the cabin, Beth had said she would come. He pushes the naïve fragment of hope from his heart. She'd promised a lot, she'd given a lot, and she'd hated herself for it.

"Her loss." Mia waves at the fans, and releases an exhausted breath. "Shit, I can't wait till we're famous and we can pay roadies to unload all this crap."

"You're an excellent roadie, don't sell yourself short."

She flashes him a you're-an-asshole-but-I-love-you-anyway glare, and heaves a case of wires from the ground.

She continues muttering as she hurries into the venue. "Most vocalists use this time to warm-up, you know."

Finn chuckles and follows after her, carrying his bass drum. "The day you actually get time to warm-up is the day it's over for every other vocalist in the world."

She grins at the compliment and leads the way through the labyrinthine corridors.

The venue is the Ritz compared to the dives they once played. It even has a dressing room, as opposed to them all taking turns getting ready in a single toilet cubicle, and only minimal brown water stains on the possibly-asbestos ceiling tiles.

"Fancy," Finn smiles as he steps inside.

A mirror surrounded by mostly-functioning light bulbs glows in the corner of the room, mounted on the bottle-green wall. One side of the room is dedicated to a giant cork board, displaying posters for upcoming local events. Vixen's Wail has the biggest poster, the most eye-catching, thanks to Nic's graphic design skills. Anya has already taken a sharpie to it and signed her name. The band's costumes, for when they hit the stage, are hung along the opposite wall, wrapped in their dry-cleaners' plastic.

Finn's throat tightens. It's hard not to feel elated. This is the payoff for a decade of hard work. It's the beginning of something big, he can feel it.

With all seven members of Vixens Wail inside, the dressing room becomes a hive of bristling energy, as they begin to prepare for the show, and as the soundcheck approaches, Beth Barlow is momentarily the furthest thing from his mind.

Eighteen

"This was a mistake." Beth tugs at the hem of the tight black leather mini-dress. "Big mistake."

The line ahead of them has barely moved since they joined it, and a voice in the back of her mind tells her to give up and go home. It's a ridiculous idea. She's been standing, shivering opposite the same office window for half an hour. The group of teenagers in front of them in the line chatter excitedly about the show, talking about their favorite songs, and which member of the band is superior to the others.

"Oh shush. You're hot," Sadie shivers beside her. Her eyes, made stunning by the expertly-applied smokey eyeshadow and winged liner, scan the line to get into the venue, as she bunches up her bare shoulders and wraps her arms around her black corseted waist. Sadie looks incredible. "He's going to dive off the stage, scoop you up in his arms and ravage you."

She dismisses Sadie with an exasperated shake of her head. "Stop." She tugs down the dress again and wraps her arms around herself.

Back in the apartment, Beth felt sexy. The dress showed off her figure perfectly, accentuating the curve of her hips and waist, but out here she feels underdressed, exposed.

Still, Sadie did a great job with her makeup; sleek eyeliner, and dark matte red lips, every bit the vampiric seductress.

But she's not there to seduce. In fact, now she's there, she can't think of a single damn reason to go through with it. All she can think about is how desperate she looks. "I'm not talking about the dress. This whole thing is a bad idea."

"What's the worst that can happen?"

"He sees me in the audience, thinks I'm stalking him, has me thrown out, finds out about the painting, files for a restraining order and I make exactly zero dollars for the charity."

Sadie blinks rapidly. "But the best case is that he sees you, realizes he was a dipshit for letting you go, and takes you backstage for an hour or two, and we meet up later when you're walking funny."

Beth gives a weak chuckle as the teenagers in front stop talking and grimace over their shoulders at the pair.

"The more likely scenario," Sadie continues, undaunted by their audience. "Is that he doesn't even see you, you realize it was just a one-night stand, he acted like an asshole, and you can finally move on."

"You're right." Beth bows her head in defeat, though her tone is dismissive. "He was an asshole. I see it now. I've seen the light. You saved me. My savior." She rolls her eyes "So, let's just go home."

As if in response, the people ahead shuffle forward. Sadie threads her arm through the crook of Beth's elbow and drags her forward as the line snakes into the venue.

"You're so full of it. We're going in," Sadie sighs. "I'll buy you an over-priced wine, and we can stand at the back and talk shit about him, but we're doing this. You can't wonder about him forever."

Beth opens her mouth to protest, but as they approach the red-brick building, and the name Vixen's Wail glows on the display above the door, her throat clenches shut.

Somewhere, deep within the building is a rhythm; a slow, steady, pounding beat. Drums. Her heart slams against her ribs in response.

She barely notices Sadie handing their tickets to the security guy on the door, barely registers when she hands him her I.D. and he secures a blue paper band around her wrist. They walk inside, and are immediately engulfed by a sea of excited fans. The theatricality of the audience is stunning. There are vampires and undertakers, ghostly brides and leather-clad phantoms, and countless people wearing Vixen's Wail shirts. The constant drone of low chatter joins the beat as they pass by the merch stall and into the vast dimly-lit hall.

The venue is already half-full. The stage at the far end is cloaked in shadow, but blue lights cast dusky twilight illumination over the audience. The heady scent of warm bodies, and the sharp tang of spilled beer cloys Beth's breaths. She scans the stage squinting at the blackness beyond the drums, but whoever is playing is completely obscured from her view.

The heat in the rapidly filling venue makes her lightheaded.

"If you don't answer me, I'm just getting you something really gross," Sadie all but yells into her ear, tightening her already vice-like grip around Beth's hand.

Beth whips around, eyes wide. "What?"

"Drink," Sadie calls over the noise. "What would you like to drink?"

More and more people are spilling through the doors. The stifling air grows heavier as though waiting for thunder to break the pressure. A group of women in their early twenties hurry past, unfolding a banner emblazoned with scarlet lettering: "We love you, Finn!"

Beth's breath catches. In this packed room, there must be close to a thousand people, and among them, so many who want him, and wouldn't pass up the chance for one passionate night with him. No wonder he cast her aside so effortlessly. He could take his pick of so many.

The whole time she's pined for him, deliberated reaching out to him, even painted him, she doubts he even thought of her. How naïve she has been to fall for a rock star.

Her jaw sets in determination. Tonight, she'll bid him goodbye. It's the last time she'll ever think of him.

She almost convinces herself.

"Wine." Her heart skips as the soundcheck ends. "Red. Absolutely enormous."

***

"This is it." Finn holds on to Mia and Jordan's hands as the band stands in a circle, heads bowed. "This night changes everything. Our first sold out gig, our biggest venue."

He tightens his grip on Jordan's shaking hand and gives her a reassuring squeeze. She forces out a slow breath, pursing her lips as she aims it down. In response, Mia runs on the spot and raises her crimson-lensed eyes to the ceiling.

The towering height of her shoes doesn't restrict the rapid pounding of her feet.

While the rest of his band get energized, Finn's heart beats steady. Beyond the stage doors, the distant racket of the audience is an oncoming storm, but he's weathered his fair share.

"Let's give them a show," Nic whispers, kohl-lined eyes screwed tight.

"Let's change their lives," Mia grins.

The circle breaks and they take up their instruments. Finn waits in the wings, sticks in hand. He'll be the first on stage, the vanguard, setting the rhythm for his bandmates to follow.

Beyond the stage, the audience cheers; a sign that the lights have dimmed, ready for his entrance. He pulls in a breath, balls his fists, and closes his eyes.

What if she is out there?

Stop. She isn't. Get over it.

He opens his eyes, shakes away any thought of Beth, and strides out onto the darkened stage, to the earth-shattering cheer of the people who love him.

Nineteen

If Beth had been preparing for weeks, she still wouldn't have been ready to see him again. Finn strides out; confident, dominating the stage with his size and that cocky grin playing across his perfect lips. If anything, he looks even better than she remembered, his black tank-top fitted tight against his broad frame, his kohl-lined eyes intense beneath the stage lights. He raises his tattooed arms toward the audience, and they erupt into adoring cheers.

Her stomach tightens. The back of her neck tingles, as though his teeth still graze against her skin.

"Fuck."

"See?" Sadie smiles as she yells over the roar of the crowd. "He's just a guy."

Beth sucks in a breath, grateful for the dim light over the audience, grateful that he's in the spotlight, dazzled, and can't see her. The venue shrinks, the crowd fades, and it's just her and him.

It's the first time she's seen him fully since the moment he left her, and every flicker and fading sensation of confusion, anger, longing, and attraction topples onto her, freezing her in place. He steps up onto a raised platform and approaches his drums, sits behind the kit and begins to play. Her heart pounds along with the rapid rhythm he sets.

This was a terrible idea.

She raises her plastic cup to her lips and takes a deep gulp of sour wine. The rest of the band charge out, and launch into their setlist. For all the complicated emotions swirling around her head, she has to admit they sound amazing.

She drinks as they play, the wine clouding her tumultuous thoughts as the band hurtle from one song to the next. The audience lap up the show, howling with fervent glee at the start of each new song, singing every word with enraptured passion.

"Mia's incredible," Sadie gushes in the momentary lull between songs. They have to basically scream down each other's ears to be heard.

Beth nods and takes a drink, draining the bottom inch of her cup. "I'm going to get another, you want one?"

Sadie shakes her head and turns her attention back to the stage.

The journey to the bar is a battle in itself. People stand, entranced, singing and pounding the air with their fists, a near impenetrable barrier. But she picks her way through, no doubt making several enemies along the way. At last, she's able to rest her elbows on the brightly lit bar.

The bartender raises his eyebrows and leans close.

"Red wine," she bellows above the music and hands him a twenty.

He glances at the blue armband around her wrist, nods

and turns his back, taking a red plastic cup from a stack in the corner.

She glances over her shoulder at the stage. Finn is completely obscured now, concealed behind the enormous drum kit, and the swirling clouds of dry ice.

The events of that night in the cabin play over and over in her mind. There was so much passion. The heat between them was blistering, burning too hot, too fast. She trusted him, let him see her completely, both physically and emotionally. He let her believe it meant something, and cast her aside the next morning.

"Bastard," she mutters. "Irritatingly handsome bastard."

The bartender brings over her cup, and disappears. Either the wine costs twenty dollars a cup, or he's kept her change as a tip.

Deflated, she stands to the side and drinks the crappy-but-apparently-expensive wine, and contemplates fighting back through the crowd toward Sadie.

A drenaline courses through his body, powered by the audience.

This is it. This is one of the shows that will define them.

The excitement gushing through his veins drives him through each song. Sweat drips down his body, the muscles in his arms and legs throb, but he keeps going.

By the time they reach the end of the setlist, he feels as though he only just got started. He sips from a bottle of water, while Mia keeps the crowd warm.

"You've been incredible tonight, my dearest mortals," Mia calls out to the audience, fully playing up to her fans' playful suspicion that she's an ancient vampire queen. "We're so happy to be home with you beautiful children of night."

He smiles, twirling the sticks between his fingers as he waits for the encore. If this is what his life amounts to, he'll be happy. He may have misfired when it came to Beth, may have given his heart foolishly to someone who saw no value in it, but he's happy. A smile pulls at his lips, and as he looks out to the audience. The lights shining on the stage make it hard to see, but the front few rows are hanging on Mia's every word. The emotion of it all overwhelms him. His vision blurs and his eyes begin to sting.

"So, a couple of weeks ago," Mia says as she paces the stage. "Finn, our darling drummer, came to me with a song..."

His pulse races as the audience cheer at the mention of his name. This isn't what they'd planned. *Cacoffiny* should be their encore.

"This song is rough, and we haven't quite got it all figured out yet, but you've been so good to us, and we love you, so we're going to play it for you tonight."

"It's not ready," he whispers, blood draining from his face as the audience erupts into an excited roar.

His head spins as Mia holds out her hand, beckoning him to come out from behind his drum kit, and Anya holds out her guitar for him to take. The crowd is so excited. He can't let them down. His legs tremble as he makes his way to the center of the stage, and stands beside Mia.

She smiles kindly, as though she knows how fast his heart is beating. "It's okay. It's a great song. They'll love it."

His fingers tremble as he puts the guitar strap over his shoulder, extending it fully to fit his frame. The heat from the stage lights blazes against his skin. He shields his eyes from the glare and waves to the audience.

Mia grins and puts the microphone to her lips. "So, you all know Finn's not great with titles." She flashes him a glance from the corner of her eye as the audience cheers. "This song is temporarily called *B.B.*"

TWENTY

Beth's heart freezes. The haze of the wine snaps away, and everything is pulled into sharp focus as he steps forward.

B.B.

It could mean anything, she tells herself.

When the music starts, it's a song she's heard before, a melody so gut-wrenchingly beautiful, it gave her pause the first time, and damn near kills her the second. It's the song he played for her while she painted him.

Mia stands beside him, tapping a rhythm on her thigh, before raising the microphone to her lips.

"What a fool I was to think you could ever love me. A fool to think you saw me."

Most of their other songs are about vampires and phantoms, but this is a song about something far worse than monsters. Every word Mia sings, etches into Beth's heart, cutting her deep, and rubbing confusion into the wound.

"Beth?" Sadie bursts through the crowd, her eyes searching. She grips Beth's arm and speaks close to her ear, but her voice sounds so distant. "Hey, come on, we should go. You don't need to hear this."

The crowd parts as Mia steps off the stage, lights following her as she walks around the hall, singing directly to their fans. Finn is the only one left on stage. His eyebrows crease as he plays, and a deep red blush blooms across his cheeks. When the song reaches its chorus, Mia may as well be singing directly to Beth.

"What made you grow so cold?

I held you all night through the worst of the storm.

Did it mean nothing to you? Love forgone.

My fool heart still longs to see your face.

But I'm ashamed. So afraid,

I was only good to keep you warm."

Through it all, Beth can't take her eyes from Finn. When he played for her that night, there were moments of intensity, brief scowls which creased his forehead, stitching together his eyebrows. But the man standing on stage looks as though he wears his frown constantly. If she didn't know better, she'd wonder if he had ever smiled. He looks…miserable. Broken.

"Beth?" Sadie tugs at her arm. "Come on, you're right, this was a mistake."

Beth can't move. It's clear his heart is broken, and she has no idea why. Was it something she did, something she said? "I think every person in here hates me right now."

"No, sweetie they don't, honestly. It's just a song. They don't know who it's about." The pitch of Sadie's voice raises, as she becomes frantic.

Beth can't take her eyes from the stage as Finn plays.

Brilliant white light dazzles her, and her vision fills momentarily with the towering silhouetted shape of Mia. The vocalist stands with Beth and Sadie, reaching out a hand toward them as she belts out the song's chorus once more.

The guitar goes silent. The song dies.

Finn stares out, his lips slowly parting as recognition flashes across his face.

The world tilts as panic rises in Beth's chest. Finn is not the only one staring. The crowd around her know something is wrong, and they turn toward the source. Her ribs close in around her lungs, and her blood flashes hot and cold.

"Shit." Finn sits backstage in the greenroom, raking his fingers through his hair.

In one moment, the night went from one of the best of his life, to a catastrophic disaster; a feeling he's becoming all too familiar with. The image of Beth, surrounded by his fans, every one of them staring at her, wondering what it was about her which rendered him completely silent. No wonder she'd bolted.

Mia sits opposite him, her forearms braced on her knees as she fidgets with a bottle of water. "I didn't know that was her. I wouldn't have—"

"I know." He releases a breath, trying to control the tremble in his fingers. "What does it mean though? Why was she here?"

The silence which follows tightens the knot in his chest. Mia shakes her head. "I don't know."

"Because she likes you," Nic cries out in exasperation. "I

told you, you heard half a phone conversation and stormed out without giving her a chance to explain."

Finn scowls. He takes the turquoise towel from around the back of his neck, and dries the sweat on his forehead. "I know what I heard."

"I love you, dude, but you're a stubborn ass." Nic sits in the seat next to him, slackening the black horsehair on the violin's bow. "I'm telling you, you need to reach out to her, and find out exactly what happened."

"And if she rejects me?"

"Then what difference does it make? At least you'd know. Then you move on having learned. But if all of this was for nothing, if you wrote that song about her going cold, when this whole time you're the one who walked out on her, then shit, do you ever have some groveling to do."

Finn stares straight ahead, his throat watertight as he picks a strand of cotton from the towel. His skin tingles with the urge to run away, hide, never show his face again. But there's also hope. A faint, flickering ridiculous hope that Nic is right.

Of course, there's also pure, cold dread which goes along with it.

He doesn't know what will happen. Doesn't know whether he's right or wrong about Beth. The only thing that's certain, is when he saw her in the crowd, one thousand people disappeared before his eyes. When he saw her, he—the man who lives and breathes noise—was silenced.

His eyes drift across the wall with the corkboard, to a poster for a charity art exhibition, to raise money for a community art center. The Grand Gallery. Friday. 8 p.m.

Tomorrow.

If he's going to do something, he needs to figure out what, and soon.

He draws a deep breath, laces his fingers on top of his head and exhales. "Ah, fuck."

Twenty-One

Humiliation leaves Beth raw. Confusion clouds her mind. The pulse in her ears, and the cold, shivery sensation of adrenaline keep her awake through the night. Every time she closes her eyes, she sees him, his pained expression. When morning comes, she's no closer to understanding what happened.

She can't stand to look at the painting of the two of them at first. It's nothing but a technicolored testament to their chaotic and brief relationship. But people are depending on her, and hopefully soon, it'll be sold.

And if no-one buys it, or if the gallery just rejects it outright, it'll make for a suitably dramatic bonfire. She wraps it carefully, and leaves it in the hallway, ready to be transported to the exhibition.

It's early evening when Sadie unlocks the door to Beth's apartment with her spare key, and creeps through the hallway to her bedroom. She peers around the door and smiles. "You okay?"

Beth grazes her lower lips with her teeth as she smooths the elegant, midnight blue dress over her hips. "Yeah."

"I'm sorry."

Taking her hand, Beth runs her thumb over her friend's knuckles. "No, don't be."

"I shouldn't have made you go last night. It was a sucky plan."

"You were only trying to help. I just wish I knew what happened. I shouldn't have left the cabin without asking him why he suddenly turned cold. I thought I could get over him, but I can't stop thinking about him."

Sadie opens her mouth to speak, but thinks better of it. It can't be anything which Beth hasn't already thought. Since she got home from the concert, an infinite loop of questions and what-ifs has plagued her. She's dissected everything from the lyrics of the song, to the look in his eyes when he saw her. None of it makes sense. It stopped making sense the moment she fell for a man she hardly knew.

"You look stunning," Sadie smiles. "At least tonight should be relatively drama free."

Beth can't help but chuckle. "Well, they don't know what I painted yet. The look on their faces will be almost as horrified as Finn's… Let's just get it over with. And you're stunning too. You always are." She draws a deep breath and forces a smile.

"I feel like I'm getting married." Finn shakes out his arms and bounces on his heels in an attempt to diffuse some of his nervous energy.

His bedroom is cluttered with discarded clothes; shirts

which looked too casual, pants which somehow didn't fully convey his feelings. He's not exactly sure of the criteria he's trying to reach, but when he gets there, he'll know.

Mia chuckles as she stands back and scrutinizes him. It's the only suit he owns, other than the one he uses solely for funerals. It has to be good enough.

"Getting married is far less terrifying than trying to find out if your feelings are reciprocated." She holds out another tie, a plain blue silk one. "Try this."

He fumbles his way through tying the knot, trying hard not to become exasperated. "How do I look?"

She tilts her head to the side. "Kind of like a big blue penguin."

"That's good," he nods, curling his fingers to stop his hands from trembling. "Maybe? She likes penguins."

Mia smiles and steps back, allowing him to see his reflection. His hair is sleek, slicked back and cropped at the sides, and his beard trimmed and smoothed down. The blue suit is snug around his arms and stomach, but it's definitely a step up from the Muppets shirt Beth first saw him in. He feels handsome, if a little stuffy.

With a smile, Mia hangs his cast-off ties back in the wardrobe and stands with her hands on her hips. "What're you going to do when you get there?"

"Uh… good question."

The tie is suddenly stifling, his plan poorly thought out. There's every chance Beth will reject him. She might be angry, hurt. She might actually hate him.

He pulls on the knot, rips away the tie and throws it onto his bed. With a huff he unfastens the top two buttons of his shirt, desperate for air. "I don't know. I don't know what I'm doing."

Frustration clenches his jaw. He's been thinking about it since last night, running over every conceivable scenario, imagining his grand entrance, what he'll say to her, how many times he'll apologize. Even the façade of dignity he'll wear if it turns out he was right all along and she doesn't want him.

But he won't know unless he tries.

He sprays cologne into the air and walks forward, spinning around like his bandmates taught him. "I'm sorry about *B.B.*"

Mia smiles. "It's okay. It was a good song, but I don't doubt you'll write more. Hopefully after tonight you'll have happier things to write about."

"Or even sadder."

"Stop," she laughs. "Don't wear the tie. It looks good without. Smart but not stuffy."

He gives a sharp nod. "Okay."

Finn steps back as she gives him one last glance over.

"Looks good. You ready?"

He isn't, and he may never be, but if not now, then he'll never know where to find her. It may already be too late. "Let's do this."

Twenty-Two

Beth's ears burn as the exhibition's curator stares, rubbing his clean-shaven cheek with wax paper fingertips.

"Not what we were expecting…" he raises his wispy grey eyebrows and turns to face her. "Certainly eye-catching. I'm sure it'll sell."

"Thank you. I hope so too." Her cheeks are scalding as she awaits his verdict.

"Put it in the main room," the curator instructs the gallery's assistants. "Well done, Ms. Barlow."

"Thank you." Beth's heart slows a little as the curator walks away. The tension in her shoulders melts as Sadie approaches with two flutes of champagne.

"Nice tits," her friend laughs, glancing at the painting as it's carried through to the main room.

Beth stifles a laugh, biting the inside of her cheek as the gallery's guests mill around. She's already noticed several people looking at her work, and a couple of them seemed interested enough to consider buying.

Sadie stands beside her, following her gaze across the lobby. "Congratulations. Are you feeling better now?"

"Calmer," Beth exhales and smiles. "I'm still confused by it all. I think I've felt every possible emotion in the past twenty-four hours. But now… standing here, with my work on the gallery's walls." She takes a sip of her champagne, letting the bubbles roll across her tongue. "This is what I always wanted. If nothing else, Finn inspired me to paint, and I'm proud of what I produced."

Sadie raises her glass. "As you should be."

They toast her achievement, and as she sips the free champagne, Beth can't help but smile.

There's a decent crowd at the gallery, and it takes Finn a little while to get in. The whole time he's in line, waiting for people's bags and coats to be checked, he scans the room, looking for a trace of her. He scours each passer-by for the gleaming waterfall of her hair, for the warmth of her smile. As he waits, dread creeps along his spine. It's fear that she isn't there, and fear that she is.

He pays the entrance fee at the door and steps inside, alone and uncertain. His heart hammers and his palms begin to sweat. What if she doesn't want him there, or she's moved on? What if she can never forgive him for last night? The terror in her eyes when he saw her at the gig haunts him.

Resisting the urge to run back outside and call Mia for a ride home, he makes his way through the gallery's side rooms, searching for her. He's out of place among this swanky crowd who stand around chatting and sipping champagne. An intruder in her world, trespassing in her realm, and there's every chance he'll be banished forever.

It's only when he steps into the central room, with its high domed ceiling, and endless echo, he sees her. Well, not *her* precisely.

A painting.

The butterflies he had in his stomach before their first kiss, return, fluttering in his stomach. They soar to his chest, their vibrations quickening the pulse in his throat. The painting is erotic, beautiful, an explosion of color and passion. There are two subjects; one is definitely her, back arched, her dark hair flying wildly, her lips parted in bliss. The other figure… he scarcely allows himself to believe it, but the tattoos are unmistakable. The other is *him*.

His heart damn near shatters as he steps closer, and the tiny copper strands in his portrait's beard glisten. The care she's taken to portray him humbles him yet again.

His eyes sting, because he sees now, exactly what he is. It's obvious in the way she painted him, the way she painted him back in the cabin. Both times her depiction shook him. And now he knows, with absolute certainty, that he's the most foolish man alive.

The entire time he's been thinking of her, she's been thinking of him. If not for his stubbornness, his fragile ego, his easily bruised heart…

He has to do something.

The laminated white tag beneath the painting reads; "*Rhythm,* Elizabeth Barlow." He smiles at the title, and at seeing her full name. There's a price listed below, one which dries out his throat, but it's worth it to try to patch the hole he's torn between them.

Twenty-Three

Beth stifles a yawn on the back of her hand, and hopes none of the artists saw. It isn't boredom. On the contrary, their work is beautiful, and it takes constant affirmation to remember that these are her peers. Her work is displayed alongside theirs.

But the excitement and the drama of the past two days have drained her, and though she's exactly where she wants to be at that moment, some part of her is already bundled up in her bed. The image of Finn onstage, his indecipherable expression, flickers through her mind, pouncing whenever her attention wanes.

She fights to concentrate on an intricate oil painting of the local farmer's market. A "sold" sign covers the price tag.

So many versions of last night's events clamor in her mind; a version where she confronted him, a version where he climbed down from the stage and swept her into his arms. That one replays most often. In that fantasy, there's no need for an explanation, no need to apologize, just swelling music, convenient wind machines, heaving bosoms…

"You okay?" Sadie asks, the toned, cool skin of her upper arm brushing against Beth's burning shoulder.

Beth takes a sip of her champagne and smiles, hoping it's convincing enough to avoid trying to explain the knotted emotions constricting her thoughts. "Mm-hm."

"Ms. Barlow?"

She flinches at the sound of her name.

The curator smiles and offers her his hand to shake. "I'm pleased to inform you your painting has sold. Congratulations, and thank you for helping our cause."

The room spins a little as Sadie grabs her arm. "That's amazing, Beth!"

"I…" Beth's throat closes as her vision pulses. It's been on display for less than ten minutes. It's a good painting, but surely not *that* good.

The curator chuckles. "The buyer actually paid double our asking price. It'll help us tremendously. And they've volunteered to teach music lessons once a week when the new center opens."

Double. Music lessons. She can barely hear the curator over the thrum of her heart. Could it have been Finn? It seems too much to hope for. She forces herself to pause, to consider every avenue. Perhaps it isn't him at all. But who else…?

"Who was it?" Sadie asks, helpfully sorting Beth's tumbling thought process into words. Her fingers dig into the flesh of Beth's forearm.

The curator chuckles. "I'd be happy to introduce you, if you'd like?" He smiles, tilting his head slightly as he waits for Beth's response.

Finn paces, back and forth, as though his footsteps could wear a trench into the gallery floor. A ditch where he can hide.

Perhaps a day will come when he actually finds the right words to say at a given moment, but it is not this day.

Hey, I bought your giant painting of us fucking, because I wanted to show you how much you mean to me, and how sorry I am for being an ass.

Hi there, remember me? The guy from the painting…

No.

Beth, I'm sorry. I… fuck…

He smooths his hair back with both hands, and pushes a breath from his tightening chest. The thought of approaching her is daunting. Perhaps she doesn't want to see him at all. Perhaps what he heard out on the balcony was true.

He turns to the wall and scours the painting, as though it holds the secret to making things right, some hidden clue she left, the key to winning her heart.

"You know, if anything, you should've gotten a discount." The familiar voice at his back sends his heart plummeting to his stomach.

He doesn't dare turn around. She can't see the blood draining from his face, the sweat prickling his hairline. "It was a small price to pay for being a total jackass."

The scent of her perfume, faint and warmed by her skin, makes his heart beat harder. Nervous energy pulses through his body, making him restless. He doesn't know what to do with his hands, or how to stand. When he planned this out, he imagined he'd feel handsome, suave, but in reality, he's clumsy, unrefined, a rough-cut slab of granite in a gallery of pristine marble statues.

"I think we should talk," she says.

Those words are almost the end of him. His heart can't settle on an emotion. Relief, at the fact she's willing to talk. Anxiety, that the talk may be their last. He messed up, and whatever she decides, he'll have to live with it. She's in control, his fate in her hands.

He turns to face her, to face his fear, and the sight of her forces the air from his lungs.

TWENTY-FOUR

Beth practiced it a hundred times on the way over to Finn, but nothing could have prepared her for the impact of seeing him. When he turns to face her, her brain flatlines. She's used to seeing him disheveled, sweating and breathless. But, standing before her, dressed in a navy-blue suit, he's cool, calm, and inconsiderately, unfairly, ungodly handsome.

The top buttons of his shirt are open, and it takes all her willpower not to look at his chest. That bastard and his hypnotic chest hair.

"Thank you," he says, and his sweet, genuine smile almost takes hold, but fades just as quickly. His deep brown eyes dart to the side. "I wasn't sure if you'd want to talk to me."

"Neither was I." She laughs quietly, and the tension between them ebbs a little.

In the corner of her eye, Sadie hovers, grinning behind her champagne glass.

Beth freezes. The realization they're standing together in

front of an enormous painting of them passionately fucking each other, sends flashes of embarrassed heat across her face.

"We should probably move elsewhere…" she raises her eyes to the painting.

"Oh," he laughs a little. "Shit, yeah. People will start asking for autographs soon."

He lets her take the lead as they walk together out of the main hall, falling in step with each other as they reach one of the quieter side rooms. For a moment, it all seems so absurd. It would be easy to forget, to be swept away by his charm, and the desire to be held in those arms once more. If she let her heart decide her actions, she'd be pressed against him, savoring the lips she's longed for since she first came to his door to complain about the noise. But she can't let her heart decide.

He doesn't speak. He waits for her.

So, she says the only thing she can think of, the only thing which conveys the complexity of her confusion, the weeks of resentment and the inexplicable desire to hang on to a man who walked away from her after one night. "Finn, what the fuck happened?"

He sinks down, sitting on a marble bench, gripping the edges as he looks up at her. "I think I might have fucked up." After a moment, a muscle flexes in his jaw, and his gaze falters. "I woke up that morning, and it was intense." He gives a quiet huff of laughter. "I was… excited, hopeful. But then I heard you talking on the phone."

Her forehead tightens as her brows knit together. "I don't understand."

"I don't know who you were talking to, but you were telling them how awful it was, how you hated yourself for it, and…I assumed you were talking about what we did."

Her silence lasts an eternity as she stares at the wall above his head. The intensity in her eyes tells him she's rifling through her memories. At last, she laughs a little in disbelief. "Finn, I think it was about the storm, and how many times I complained about your drums."

He pauses and blinks as his cheeks darken. "Shit."

"Why didn't you just talk to me?"

"I don't do the one-night-stand thing, and even though we had an incredible night, we were still pretty much strangers. When I heard you, my pride took over. I panicked. I shut you out before you could say anything else, and I know that was the wrong thing to do." He stands, and she's almost startled by the size of him. "I messed up. I know I did. And I'm so sorry, because it must've been confusing, and embarrassing and hurtful, and you didn't deserve a moment of it." He stops and draws a breath. "I wish more than anything I'd spoken to you, because I hope…" His throat bobs as he swallows, and he seems to shrink before her eyes.

Beth presses her fingertips to her lips, concealing her smile. "Look, that night… us… none of it made sense. I've spent every day since trying to unravel it, figure out how something can go from feeling so completely right, to so catastrophically wrong."

He nods once, pressing his lips together. "I believe the key ingredient is an enormous dipshit."

"More like two." She chuckles. "Well, at least you didn't paint us having sex."

"That's true. Score one for me. But on the other hand, you didn't just pay a fortune for a giant painting of yourself having sex, hoping it would come off as some grand gesture." The corners of his eyes crease as he slips his hands into his pants pockets. "Oh, by the way, the song, the one you heard last night—we aren't playing it again, ever. It's gone."

"You didn't have to."

"No, it's okay. I'll come up with something new."

His smile melts her, demolishing the last remnants of her resolve. They share the silence, at peace in each other's company as the world continues turning around them.

***

Finn doesn't know *how* it worked out, only that it did. Every smile she gives him is a goddamn miracle, far more than he ever dared to hope for. His heart is all but bounding, and he swears to himself, over and over that he'll never mess this up again.

"Can I get you a drink to celebrate your sale?" His cheeks hurt from smiling so hard.

"I actually came here with a friend. I don't want to leave her alone for too long. Besides, you've spent more than enough tonight." She flashes him a grin. "But, there's a free champagne bar for artists. I can stealthily get you a drink to celebrate your extravagant purchase." He's burning up in her presence, following after her like a giddy puppy as she all but glides toward the bar. She glances at him over her shoulder. "What are you going to do with the painting anyway?"

"I have absolutely no idea. I didn't exactly plan this."

"You don't have to keep it." She passes him a flute of champagne, her eyes meeting his and making the butterflies in his stomach soar.

The glass feels so tiny in his hands. He takes a sip, and tries not to grimace at the taste. "I want to. Uh… if that's okay?"

She clinks her glass against his and smiles. "It's all yours." Her eyes brighten as they slide across to someone behind him. "This is Sadie, my friend."

When she approaches, he shakes the new woman's hand, but his mind races. She's introducing him to her friend. That's good… right? Unless her friend knows what an ass he was. Oh shit.

"Hey," he smiles. "Finn."

"I know," the woman says, her eyes narrowing as she looks at Beth. "Is he off the hook?"

Beth scowls for a moment, letting him marinade in the tension. When she laughs, it's the loveliest thing he's ever heard. "Yeah. It's all good."

"Oh, thank fuck," Sadie grins. "I'm a huge fan. Huge. Love *Cacoffiny*."

He draws a dramatically sharp breath. "Me too!"

And then, as though it's the simplest, most natural thing in the world, Beth's fingers press against his palm and slide down to lace with his. For the first time in a while, the warmth in his chest isn't from embarrassment, or nerves, but the glow of a fire which has found the best place to burn.

Twenty-Five

Sadie and Finn chatter away about Vixen's Wail as the three of them sit snugly in the back of a cab. Their burgeoning friendship makes Beth happy, but the question of what will happen once Sadie gets out at her home weighs heavy in the back of her mind.

They've held hands all night, laughed and talked and exchanged glances which ignited fire in the pit of her stomach, but there's always the possibility he wants to take it slow. She wouldn't mind, and without a doubt he's worth the wait, but if that's the case, she's going to have to figure out how to get an industrial sized shipment of batteries.

The cab's brakes squeak as it comes to a stop outside Sadie's house. "It was awesome to meet you, Finn." She grins as she collects her purse and opens the door. "Be good to her, okay?"

"Of course," Finn smiles and waves as she closes the door.

The meaning behind Sadie's grin isn't subtle at all. She turns on her heel and heads up her driveway.

Finn releases a heavy breath as the cab pulls away, and his grip on Beth's hand tightens. "That was terrifying."

Beth chuckles. "Sadie?"

"Yeah." He turns toward the window, his throat flexing as he swallows.

"You did good. She likes you." He turns to face her, and knocks the air from her lungs. She'll never get used to how handsome he is. Her eyes drift down to his lower lip, soft and unfairly suckable. God, she misses it. "Not as much as I like you."

"Good to know."

He holds her gaze and the air in the cab grows thick.

Just ask him. The worst he can say is no.

"Do you…" Her stomach tenses as his thumb strokes her finger. Her pulse beats in her throat, her vision darkens, and her mouth dries as she summons the courage to ask. "My place?"

His lips part a little as his breath stalls. He gives a barely-perceptible nod. "Sounds good."

The rest of the ride home passes agonizingly slow. Anticipation blurs the time, spreading seconds into minutes into eternities. The whole time she can't stop thinking about him, his body, his touch, his lips. By the time they pull up outside her apartment, she's so turned on she can barely think straight.

She pays the driver, because Finn has already spent too much, and leads him into the building, her body aching as they wait for the elevator.

"It takes forever," she chuckles to fill the silence.

"It's worth the wait."

Her body burns as he takes her hand and raises it to his lips. The bristles of his beard tickle her knuckles as he kisses the back of her hand. His lips linger, and when his warm, brown eyes meet hers, she can hardly breathe. The warmth and softness of his mouth brings back memories of that night, and if the elevator doesn't get there soon, she'll pick him up and damn well carry him up the stairs to her apartment.

The elevator's cheerful *ding* makes her jump. The doors slide open and they step inside. It takes her a moment to remember which floor she's lived on for the past seven years.

By the time they get upstairs she doubts she'll even remember her own name. At least, she hopes not.

They step into the elevator, and Finn can't help but look at them both in the mirrored wall. He takes it as a sign that they both wore nearly the same shade of blue, that they look so darn sweet together.

She takes his breath away in her dress, but then, she looks incredible in pajamas when she's just woken up, or wrapped up in a coat, telling him to be quiet.

Her hesitation before pressing the button to her floor sows a seed of doubt in the back of her mind. Maybe she doesn't want this after all.

He clears his throat, and tries not to sound disappointed. "Are you okay?"

She gives a breathless chuckle. "Oh, yeah. Sorry."

Her thumb jabs the button for the fifth floor.

As the doors close, she steps beside him, the heat from her body pulsing against him. His knees nearly buckle as she smooths the lapel of his jacket. Her fingers are trembling. She turns back to the mirror and smiles. "You're so handsome."

Her words wind him. For the first time that night, he lets go of her hand, and steps behind her, maintaining eye contact through their reflections. She leans back, her ass pressing against his hips, and the proverbial ropes binding him, holding him back from bending her over and fucking her right there in the elevator, are frayed to nothing but threads.

He bows his head, breathing in the intoxicating scent of her. He wants to kiss every curve, and every inch of her soft, warm body. There's over a month of time to make up for, so many nights of wishing and hoping, and he intends to show her how sorry he is for each and every one.

"You're the most beautiful woman in the world," he whispers, her neck agonizingly close to his lips.

Her eyes close and lips part as his fingers glide to her waist, pulling her close to him, teasing them both. His breath staggers as she raises her arms, giving him full access to her body. It takes all his willpower not to grasp at her, to fill his hands with her soft, beautiful breasts. His cock is rock solid against her ass.

The elevator jolts as they reach her floor, and as the doors slide open, every atom in his body is burning for her.

Twenty-Six

Beth's entire body pulses as they make their way to her door. The corridors in her apartment complex are now irritatingly and unfairly long and winding. Finn laces his fingers with hers as she leads him through the labyrinth.

"It's just down here," she says, picking up her pace.

They're almost breaking into a run as they near her apartment. He wraps his arms around her waist, kissing her neck as she fumbles with her key.

"You're distracting." Every kiss sends tingles through her body.

"I try to be."

At last the door unlocks and they step into her apartment. Having him there takes a moment to adjust to, as every fantasy she's had for the past few weeks becomes a reality.

As the door closes, she presses her back to the hallway wall and grips the lapels of his jacket, pulling him onto her. The weight of him, pressing against her against the wall sets her aflame. Heat courses through her body as his lips linger half an inch from hers.

His eyes close as he leans in, and the moment their lips touch, the fire consumes her. She can't hold back, tugging his lower lip between her teeth, coaxing a groan from him as he takes her wrists in his hands and holds them to the wall above her head.

His cock is hard against her stomach as he kisses her, pinning her between the wall and his soft, yet sturdy body. She never wants to be anywhere else.

He shrugs off his jacket, letting it fall to the floor as he sinks to his knees. Her breath hitches as he pushes up her skirt, his hands gliding along her legs, exposing her inch by inch. Anticipation tightens a knot in the base of her stomach.

She runs her fingers back over his hair as he bunches the fabric of her skirt at her hips. Her breath comes in ragged, stilted bursts as he works slowly, cherishing every second of her arousal. He bites his lower lip as he slides her underwear down to her thighs.

"You're so beautiful," he whispers, glancing up at her. "I've thought about this every night since I last saw you."

"Me too."

"I'm going to do everything I can to make this past month up to you."

The moment his tongue slides against her clit she cries out, thrusting her hips toward him. She presses her head against the wall, gasping with every long, slow, stroke of his tongue. Her legs almost give out, and she has to steady herself on his shoulders.

The rasp of his beard against her thighs, the warmth and softness of his lips and tongue; it's as perfect as it is devastating. He savors every inch of her, moaning as though he'd happily spend all night licking her, pinning her to the wall until she forgets everything but his name and the sensation of his mouth on her tender skin. She has to constantly remind herself that her neighbors are close, the walls are thin, and that she has to keep breathing.

As good as it feels, it isn't easy for her to climax while standing. Each time she becomes overwhelmed or over-sensitive, he stops and lets her come down to earth. In those pauses he kisses the tops of her thighs, her hips, her belly, until she tangles her fingers in his hair and directs him back to her pussy.

When her knees begin to tremble and she can feel herself getting close, Finn increases the pressure. His tongue works her faster, faster, until she shatters, her orgasm raging through her. She buries her fingers in his tousled hair, holding his face to her, as his tongue draws out every last pulse of pleasure coursing through her body.

She comes back down slowly, pressing her head to the wall. Through the haze, she can see he's standing, watching her with that cocky, irresistible grin she's both riled by and can't live without.

He takes her hands, and once more pins them above her head, and kisses her. She tastes herself on his tongue, the heady taste of arousal, and she wants more. When he breaks away from her lips, he kisses her jaw, working his way down her neck, to her shoulders. Every kiss is an apology, and an oath that this time he won't walk away. Neither will she.

She gasps as he lifts her into his arms, holding her to him.

"Bedroom," he whispers. "I need you."

He doesn't need to say it twice.

He'll spend the rest of his life making her feel good if she'll let him.

Finn's heart is racing as he carries her in his arms as she directs him to the bedroom. Every inch of her apartment is her; her art on the walls, ongoing projects set up in nearly every room, pictures of herself, her family and friends.

He allows himself a shred of hope, that perhaps one day their homes will merge, and he'll write music while she paints. The animal part of his brain is quieted for a moment as he lets himself imagine what could come next.

They only make it halfway through the apartment before she's unbuttoning his shirt, kissing every bared inch of his skin and sending shivers through his body.

"I've never felt like this before." He can't keep the words locked inside. He almost lost her once because he didn't speak his mind, and he isn't going to let that happen again. "I couldn't stop thinking about you."

"Neither could I." She runs her hands over his body, touching him as though she's making up for lost time too; hungry, desperate.

He could swear he's glowing, shining from the inside out. "I never want there to be a day I don't see you."

She pauses, her eyes searching his, and for a moment, he wonders if he said something wrong. If he came on too strong too soon.

"There won't be." She nestles against him, tugging his earlobe with her teeth. "I'm yours."

By the time he reaches her bedroom he can barely contain himself. The sensation of having her in his arms again is overwhelming, and the ferocious need to have her takes over.

They stumble together onto the bed, tearing at each other's clothes. Their lips, tongues and teeth take anything they can, licking, biting, kissing every inch of skin.

He loves her body, so soft and full. Her curves are mesmerizing, addictive, and he can't stop kissing them. He loves the taste of her. When he slides his cock into her, his entire body shudders with pleasure. She clings to him, nails raking his shoulders, legs wrapped around his waist as though she can't bear the thought of him pulling away from her. He would never.

Won't ever.

Sparks burst behind his eyelids as he grinds his hips against hers, moving slowly, making sure she feels every inch of him filling her.

"Oh—God yes," she gasps, tilting back her head as her lips form around a silent cry.

"You feel so goddamn good."

He could spend a lifetime like this, lost in her, his body tingling with the sensation of her. She meets his thrusts with her own, rolling her hips beneath him so he can hardly think straight. Hot and snug and so fucking wet, both from his mouth and her own arousal. And he can't hold back; wants to make it last but he can't. Her grip on his shoulders loosens as he quickens his pace, thrusting into her with that savage, primal rhythm that first drove them together.

"You're mine," she gasps, wrapping her hands around his biceps, running her nails across the ink on his skin, a little pain to heighten the pleasure.

"All yours."

Finn's breath quickens as he fucks her, harder, deeper,

loving everything about her from her moans to the way her tits bounce in time with his hips. Her teeth graze her lower lip as she whispers his name.

It's too much, too good. He thrusts deep into her as he comes, his back arched and belly pressed into hers as wave after wave of pleasure rolls through him.

Beth stroked her hand down the center of his chest, chuckling as he shivers through the last pulses of his orgasm.

"Good?" she asks playfully.

"Uh-huh," he manages to say before his arms turn to spaghetti and he collapses onto her, wedging his face between her breasts and kissing the space between them.

She threads her fingers through his hair and holds him, her heart slowing beneath his cheek.

"Don't get too relaxed," he says. "I'm not done with you yet."

He raises his head to flash her a grin, but the look in her eyes knocks the air from his lungs. Tender and content and so goddamn happy. And his. Every bit as besotted as he is. Every bit as whole.

He loves everything about her, everything she is and will ever be. And though a part of him knows it's too soon, but he can't help it. He loves *her*.

He doesn't say it, not aloud, but he damn well spends all night showing her.

Epilogue

Two months ago, if you'd asked Beth what she thought of Finn Tovey, she'd have told you he was loud, smug, and irritatingly handsome. None of that has changed.

As she watches him from the side of the stage, she can't help but smile. He's hers. She's his. And she's all but glowing with pride as he plays.

The art center's first public exhibition almost kept her from the show, but seeing him in his element, unaware that she's there, makes all the rushing around worthwhile.

The audience roar the words along with Mia as Vixen's Wail blasts through the final song of the evening. Another triumphant sold-out show for an enraptured audience.

Beth can't take her eyes off him as he pounds the drums, biceps flexing, skin shining with sweat. Her fingers flex with the desire to touch him, to have him. They haven't said it to each other yet, but she loves him. She loves him so much, and she's just about done with playing it cool.

The song ends, and he bows to the audience, throwing

out his battered sticks. Her heart pounds as he turns to her, the aftershocks of the thundering rhythm of his drums.

"You're incredible," she beams as he hurries toward her with a wide grin. "The new stuff sounds amazing."

He takes one of her hands in both of his, and brings it to his lips, sending a flurry of excitement coursing through her. "Really? I was distracted by the gorgeous woman watching me from the wings during the last few songs." He takes a towel from one of the backstage staff and wipes the perspiration from his face. "How was the gallery?"

"Good. There are a lot of talented young people in this town." She follows him into his personal dressing room. "They're excited to see you there tomorrow. I think your lessons are their favorite part."

He beams as he collapses on a brown leather couch. She stands back, giving his time and space for the adrenaline of the show to run its course, and admiring the body she can't get enough of.

He sits with his legs spread wide, one elbow resting on the arm of the couch as he takes deep breaths. It takes all her willpower not to climb on top of him.

When she meets his eyes, he's looking at her, his gaze soft, his lips parted a little. He stands and steps toward her, and her body tingles in his presence.

"Hey," he reaches out, brushes a strand of hair back from her face and tucks it behind her ear, sending bolts of electricity across her skin. "There's something I want to tell you, and I've been waiting for the right time, but nothing seemed good enough to tell you—"

"Is it that you love me?" She grins as he freezes. "Because if it is, I know, and I love you too."

"Yeah," he chuckles. "I guess it really is that simple. I love you."

She raises onto her tiptoes, pulling him toward her as she melts against his kiss. She wouldn't exchange all the quiet in the world for this.

He pulls away, his chest slowly heaving and eyes glassy, as he slowly peels off his sweaty black tank top. "I never want to be without you, Beth."

"Me neither," she grins, her teeth sinking into her lower lip as her eyes feast on the sight of his bare torso. "But you're still not bringing the spare drum kit to my apartment."

His smile widens as he crouches and lifts her over his shoulder. She laughs as he carries her over to the shower in the corner of the dressing room.

"You wouldn't dare," she shrieks as she dangles upside down, swatting his ass as he turns on the steaming jet of water. "Finn, I swear I'll bite you."

"I'm counting on it," he says as he sets her back down, and she doesn't have time to draw breath before he's kissing her, his hands pulling at her clothes.

That irresistible bastard.

This is it, their rhythm, and damn, they play so well together.

Finn knows she's watching him as he showers. And he knows she wishes it was her hands lathering up his body. Usually, he takes his time getting clean after a show, but he can't stand to be away from her. Not tonight. She said she loves him.

She *loves* him.

Nothing can take the smile from his face as he rinses off. He can hardly believe it, and yet, he's known for almost the whole time they've been together.

"What's funny?" Beth asks, unashamedly letting her eyes wander over his naked body as he steps out of the shower. Despite her casual tone, her cheeks are pink and her eyes dark.

He shrugs, pulling a soft blue towel around his hips. "That this all started out with a noise complaint, and that's exactly what our neighbors will be doing tonight before I'm through with you."

"Oh," she narrows her eyes and purses her lips. "Smooth."

He flashes her a grin before he begins to dry off. In his heart, he knows she's the one. She's the one he'll ask to marry someday, the one he'll grow old beside.

Their hearts beat to the same rhythm, and it's a song he'll happily dance to for the rest of his life.

Sneak Preview

Keep reading for an exclusive preview of *Strings*, the next installment in the Vixens Rock series...

Strings

She's a horrible person. The absolute worst.

Sitting in a gorgeous converted barn at a round, lavishly decorated table, listening to heartwarming speeches and already halfway through her third glass of prosecco, Jordan should be happy. Fairy lights twinkle on the walls, and the warm air is scented with the gentle sweetness of dried flower bouquets. She's surrounded by friends and one of them—one of her very best friends in fact— just got married to an amazing woman.

But the way Finn smiles, the way his eyes crease as he looks at his new bride, Beth, seeing his broad chest expand with pride and adoration, turns Jordan's heart hollow.

As she stands for the toast, she smooths her hand over the curve of her hip, pushing a crease out of her dark green velvet gown. She chose the color because it popped with her lavender hair and the cool tone of her pale skin, but now… well, it's a little too on the nose.

For the past ten years, she has been Vixen's Wail's cellist. Throughout all of it, Finn has played his drums behind her.

A decade of friendship, of touring the country, and never once has she felt anything like this toward him.

She helped him prepare for the big day, accompanied him to pick out his suit and helped him rehearse his vows. She never expected to feel jealous. Never once did she see what she sees today.

Yes, she had always known Finn was handsome.

Sure, his smile makes her smile.

Okay, she looked forward to each day they'd get to hang out together… but this. This is unexpected. And it's torture.

She exhales sharply, raising her glass to toast the couple. Regardless of her unwelcome and absurd new feelings, she hopes they have a long and happy life together; she really does.

"It's so beautiful." Mia smiles beside her as the guests sit back down. The band's lead singer sets her glass on the table and reaches beneath to hold her husband's hand. "Beth's gown is gorgeous, isn't it? Let's get married again."

August's eyes soften as he turns to his wife. "Okay."

"Okay?"

"What my queen wants, my queen gets."

The couple chuckle together and though it's undeniably sweet, Jordan averts her eyes before they kiss. But of course, since it's a wedding, there are couples everywhere.

On the next table one of Finn's cousins sits whispering with his girlfriend, his fingers stroking the underside of her forearm. He's big and bearded too, a former fire watchman who found his soulmate while she was lost in the forest. Finn had told the band the story one night after practice, his eyes lighting up with a newly cemented belief that no matter the odds, if people are meant for each other, the universe will bring them together.

If only she'd known that maybe the right person was right there, all this time.

"You okay?" Mia places her hand on Jordan's forearm and gives her a gentle squeeze. "You're a thousand miles away."

"Yeah." Her throat is rough. She tries to clear it without sounding too obvious. "Just… It's been a long day."

"Weddings always are." Mia stands. Though her wedding look is a little more toned down than her onstage appearance, she's still every part the majestic goth queen. Her hair is braided tightly and dyed a vibrant midnight blue, and her black, mermaid-tail dress hugs her figure perfectly. She casts her deep brown eyes over Jordan's half-empty glass and the empty one beside that. "Don't forget we're playing tonight."

Jordan nods reassuringly, hoping Mia can't somehow tell that she absolutely did forget. Vixen's Wail are playing a three-song set after sundown. She reaches for a water jug and fills an empty glass. There's no way she's playing this set tipsy, not with emotions running so high.

"Water already, Jordo?"

The voice at her back straightens her spine and sends heat flooding across her skin. Finn stands behind her, embracing Mia.

Okay, she can do this. He's still just Finn, still her friend. She won't let misguided desire spoil that.

Despite her nerves and the turmoil raging through her heart, she turns and smiles. "You don't want me pulling the focus from you by falling off the stage during our set, now do you?"

Finn laughs, an easy, inviting sound which warms her heart. "At this point, we'll take all the free entertainment we can get."

"I warned you, weddings are expensive," Mia smiles.

When Mia steps back and takes her seat once more, Finn glances up at his new wife, as though if he looks away for too long, he'll find out she was a figment of his imagination.

"It's worth it," he says.

Jordan's eyes begin to burn and her vision blurs. "I'm so happy for you," she manages to stay before her throat closes. She clears it again and offers Finn a smile. She's absolutely not doing this.

"Thank you," Finn says warmly. When he places his hand on her bare shoulder and offers her a friendly squeeze, the warmth of his rough hands on her skin makes her heart flutter. He inhales sharply. "Oh, Mia, before I forget, I placed the ad for the vocalist like we talked about."

"Thank you." Mia smiles and raises her glass. "But stop working, enjoy your day."

"Vocalist?" Cold fear trails down Jordan's back. Her breath catches in her throat as she turns to face Mia. "You're leaving?"

"Fuck no," Mia laughs. "No, we have a few duets written for the new album. We're just looking for a guest vocalist."

Jordan breathes a little easier. The last thing she wants is for the band to split. Getting to work with her best friends, following her dreams, it's more than she ever hoped possible, even if they are still mostly playing venues with leaky ceilings and peeling paint.

Finn stands to his full height. "I'll catch you later. I want to try and get round to thanking everyone before the set."

"Yeah, see you later, Finn." Trying not to watch him leave, Jordan picks up a napkin and distracts herself by folding it into a floppy origami fortune teller.

She hopes it's a temporary crush, and not something

she'll have to deal with at every rehearsal, every performance, every night she lies alone.

Unwelcome thoughts haunt her. If only she'd realized sooner, before he met Beth. If only there was a way to reboot a heart, to factory reset her feelings. But there isn't.

Frustrated, she scrunches the napkin origami and raises her eyes. Mia is watching her.

"I need to go to the restroom," the vocalist says with a smile. "Will you come with me?"

Anything to distract her from these inconvenient, unfair feelings. They head to the bathroom together and it isn't until the door is closed behind them, and Mia has checked both stalls to make sure no one is there to hear, that Jordan realizes anything's wrong.

"Something's upsetting you," Mia states, folding her arms across her chest.

Jordan leans back against the sink countertop and mirrors Mia's gesture. "It's nothing."

"No, no it's definitely something, and if it's what I think it is, you need to put a stop to it now."

"I—"

"He's married," Mia sighs.

She could deny it, but she has never been a convincing liar. Evidently her covert lingering gazes weren't quite as secretive as she thought. "I know."

"How long have you felt this way?"

Jordan laughs quietly. "About five hours. I think. Maybe I felt something for longer, but I didn't know what it was until —" She shakes her head, laughing bitterly. "Until I saw him standing at the end of the aisle and wished, just for a moment, that I was the woman he was waiting for. And now I can't stop thinking about it."

Mia exhales heavily, drumming her matte, blood red nails against the warm, deep brown skin of her arm, fixing Jordan in an unwavering stare. "Jord—"

"I just…God, I want someone to look at me the way he looked at Beth when she was walking down the aisle." Defeated, Jordan sighs and lowers her gaze to the floor. "I know, I'm a shitty person."

"You're not. You're a good person, but your heart is acting like a total jackass." Mia laughs a little and Jordan can't help but smile at the absurdity of it. "You can't have Finn, love."

"I know. And I'd never try to. It's not something I have any intention of acting on, but…I didn't expect it to hurt."

Mia's lean arms envelop Jordan, and her senses flood with the gentle honeyed scent of the vocalist's perfume as she stands there and lets herself be held. It's been a long time since anyone hugged her. Her touch-starved heart draws on the warmth of Mia's embrace.

The vocalist releases a heavy sigh. "I hate to bring this up, but you remember you swore never to get involved with another band member. Ever."

Of course she does. Danny was the love of her life for all of three months almost a decade ago. He was the band's guitarist, tall and bearded with long silky black hair which he would throw around while he played. Their relationship had been short and scorching, but the intensity of their breakup has almost burned up the whole band. She'd sworn then and there she would never date another musician, especially not a Vixen.

Jordan nods and sighs. "I know."

"Finn is nothing like him, but this would be even messier. If you want my advice, you need to find a way to forget about these feelings." Mia steps back and checks her makeup in the mirror above the sink. As always, it's perfect. "As your friend, I'm telling you this is unhealthy and it's unfair to both of you."

"You're right."

Mia smiles and holds Jordan's gaze, her eyes intense. "And as a Vixen, I'm telling you to snap the fuck out of it. Find someone to flirt with, or just hang out with us and try not to dwell on it. If you keep thinking about Finn, at best you'll torture yourself, at worst you'll destroy your friendship with him and tear the band apart."

Jordan nods and pulls in a deep breath, before turning to look at herself in the mirror. She looks good, great, even. The green dress hugs her curves and her long, lavender hair makes her feel like a mermaid. Like a siren.

Rubbing a miniscule speck of mascara from beneath her lower eyelashes, she stands upright, pulls her shoulders back and sets her mind. She's going to get over Finn, no matter what. Keeping Vixen's Wail together is far more important than her ill-advised crush.

"You look perfect," Mia smiles. "Do whatever you've got to do to get over this."

Awkward doesn't cover it.

Étienne stands, surrounded by complete strangers, all dressed up in his best suit and left alone. Like an abandoned dog tied up outside a store. A very sparkly, extravagant store.

The same unwelcome thought that's been milling through his head all day pushes to the forefront of his mind. Getting stood up always sucks, but when your date ducks on her own cousin's wedding to avoid seeing you, it's pretty mortifying.

As a wedding singer—or rather *former* wedding singer— he's used to the environment, but of course, in the past he was always invited to be there. He doesn't know the bride or groom at this one, and he doubts they even noticed him. He was supposed to be a plus one. Now, he's a lonely loser tres- passing on these strangers' special day.

He shifts his weight as he stands behind the groom, waiting for him to finish speaking to a table of guests. Every minute he stands there feels like an eternity.

God, he hopes the guy is the gentle sort of giant. He's almost a foot taller than Étienne and built like a slab of gran- ite, but he has to say something. For goodness' sake, he was dragged into the group photos after the ceremony, placed on the front row since at five foot five he's considerably shorter than the groom's family of colossi.

Étienne's gaze trails across the party, overwhelmed by the mass of strangers. There isn't a single familiar face in the crowd. Not one.

Some of the guests glance over at him, and a few of them look again. He basks in the boost to his temporarily wounded self-esteem. Years of performing on stage have taught him how to hold himself, how to project confidence and sex appeal. It helps that he's fully aware of how hand- some he is; the way his dark lashes frame his blue-grey eyes, the way he's completely comfortable with his height and his sturdy, heavyset body. Étienne is used to being watched and wanted.

But his breath catches as one particular woman works her way across the room, sidling past the tables and chattering guests. Her full, curvaceous figure is wrapped in green velvet, and her lavender hair tumbles down her back in shimmering waves. She looks up, and his stomach flutters.

For a moment he thinks her eyes are on him, but no. It's the groom she's looking at as she takes her seat and sips a glass of water. Interesting. It seems like there's history there, but he has never really been one for drama.

He turns away and resumes his watch of the big man's back.

At last, the groom turns and looks down at Étienne. His welcoming smile falters as his eyes narrow at the intruder. "Hi. Sorry, I don't think I know you."

Clearing his throat, Étienne feels his blood run cold. "Ah, no. Um, I was supposed to be Krista's date—"

"Beth's cousin?"

"Right. Only she hasn't shown up, so I'm just, you know…"

The groom's eyebrows raise a little as he inflates his massive chest with a long breath.

Étienne braces himself. "I didn't think it was a good idea to tell Beth, you know, just in case she's upset over Krista." He pauses a second, waiting for the groom's reaction. The man's eyes flicker over to his new wife, before he gives a gentle nod. Okay, good, that was the right decision. Étienne clears his throat. "Anyway, I just came over to apologize for intruding and wish you a happy marriage."

The groom laughs a little, running his hands over the coarse hair of his beard. "That sucks man, I'm sorry."

"Yeah," Étienne sighs, giving a little breathless laugh of his own. "To be honest, I feel like a complete loser."

He feels worse than that, honestly. The week started out with the catastrophic implosion of his band, his life's meaning for almost six years. Things had been a little rocky over the past few months, but he'd hoped they could work it out. They were good, really good, but personalities weren't compatible, especially not with his guitarist.

Getting the date with Krista was the light at the end of a very bleak tunnel, but now…he's dateless and bandless. "I'm going to head on home, but I hope you all have a great evening."

"You can stay if you want?" The groom shrugs and chuckles. "Your food and drinks are already paid for and I'm sure Beth isn't going to mind. Hell, you can eat Krista's too."

It's Étienne's turn to laugh as he scans the room. The other guests are chatting, smiling, and sipping free wine. He has nothing else planned. "It wouldn't be weird?"

The groom scoffs lightheartedly. "Not at all, the more the merrier. Fill your boots."

It's easy to like this guy. Right away Étienne can tell he's one of those people with the ability to make anyone feel instantly welcome, like they've been friends for years.

"Alright, thank you."

The groom shakes his hand and the rough calluses on his palms grate against Étienne's. He remembers vaguely, Krista telling him her cousin was marrying a drummer. Working with a guy that laid back would be easy. He highly doubts the groom is going to want to talk shop on his wedding day, but putting out some feelers for musicians can't hurt.

"I'm Étienne, by the way."

"Finn. It's good to meet you."

"Can I get you a drink?" Étienne chuckles. "A drink you've already paid for."

Finn smiles and looks around the room, assessing the guests he hasn't yet spoke to. He looks happy, but exhausted.

His broad shoulders relax. "Yeah, man. A drink sounds great."

Étienne leads the way, his mind whirring. Good drummers can be hard to find and if he's to put together a new band, finding his way into Finn's good books isn't a bad idea.

"Krista mentioned you're a drummer."

"I'm surprised she knows that much," Finn sighs, relieved as he slides onto a tall wooden stool at the bar. "But yeah." He glances at the bartender. "Scotch on the rocks please."

"Same, please," Étienne nods. He's not even a whisky drinker, hates the stuff, but he'll make an exception if endears Finn to him. "Who do you play with?" He tries to sound casual, but his heart picks up its pace as anticipation settles on his chest.

The ideal answer is 'no one'. He'll take a 'yeah but they suck.' The worst possible answer would be—

"Vixen's Wail."

It's hard not to look crushed as the bartender pours their drinks. He's heard that name a few times, seen their posters around town. They're solid. Damn good vocalist too by all accounts. Their logo may as well be a huge no poaching sign.

"What do you do?" Finn asks.

"For a living?"

"Yeah."

Étienne takes a sip of the bitter, burning liquid. "Right now, not a whole lot. I'm a vocalist, but…you know, hard to be a front man with no band."

"Oh, I'm sorry, that sucks."

"This whole week sucks." Étienne takes another drink and tries not to cough as he swallows. The taste makes his eyes water. "I'm sorry. I shouldn't be complaining to you on your wedding day."

Finn drinks too, tightening his lips over his teeth as he swallows. He frowns a little, milling something over in his mind before he speaks again. "Are you looking for someone to play with?"

A spark of hope begins to smolder in his chest. "You know someone?"

"We're actually looking for a vocalist to work with us on a few duets. Nothing full-time, but if you want to audition—"

"I do." Étienne knows he should play it cool, but a chance to work with Vixen's Wail could be the start of an exciting chapter of his career. His old band never played their own music. As much as he enjoyed those crowd pleasers, singing original songs is his dream.

Finn chuckles. "Hey, that's the second time someone's said that to me today."

It's impossible not to smile. This big, beautiful bastard is throwing him a lifeline, despite the fact he's a total stranger who effectively crashed his wedding. He could hug him. "Are you sure? I mean, the type of music I usually sing isn't exactly… What is it that Vixen's Wail plays?"

"Symphonic metal."

"Right…" Étienne nods, but he hasn't a clue what any of that means. "I'm generally more of an 80s bops kind of guy."

"Are you good though?"

The question takes him aback. "Well, yeah but—"

"We're playing a set in about half an hour," Finn says. He pulls his phone out of his pocket and opens the contacts before handing it to Étienne to add his details. "Take a listen, see if you think it's something you can do and I'll text you the time and date and what's expected. The details are also on our website, you know, in case I forget." He raises his glass and grins. "To fated meetings."

Étienne doesn't want to let this guy see his hands tremble, but he can't help it. He's all but vibrating out of his damn skin with excitement as he puts in his number. The biggest gig his band ever played was as a support act for a marginally popular local band, but Vixen's Wail are on the cusp of a breakthrough. Their fans are loyal, selling out venues. This is big. Raising his glass to clink it against Finn's, Étienne can't help but smile. "To whatever comes next."

They drink together, and Étienne's body shivers at the bitter taste. When he finally gets about half the drink down, he slams it back on the bar.

Finn grins and shakes his head. "You don't have to drink it, dude. Let me get you something you actually like."

Relieved, Étienne sighs and picks up the short and sweet cocktail menu from the bar.

Acknowledgments

A lot has changed since the first time these books were in print, and there are certain people I could not have done this without.

As always, I want to give an enormous thank you to my husband, Jake. You truly are the most incredibly supportive and lovely person in the world, and I love you with all my heart.

Thank you to Janel for your kindness and support, and for picking me up when I'm feeling down.

Thank you to Emily, Allie, and Sarah for sprinting with me, and for all the laughs and pep talks.

Thank you to all my lovely patrons over on Patreon, including the Vixens For Life, Emily H, Katie B, Melanie, Linda W, Janel A, Deanna S, and D Mayo-Wells. Your support means the world to me and I couldn't have done this without you.

And thank you from the very bottom of my heart to every one of you who read this book. I can't wait to share more stories with you and your support means the world to me. If you could spare the time to leave a review I would be so grateful.

About Marie Lipscomb

Marie specializes in writing romances with plus sized heroines and plus sized heroes. She is the author of the *Hearts of Blackmere* and *Vixens Rock* series as Marie Lipscomb, and also writes short, bonkers, high-heat romances including *No Getting Ogre You* and *Santa Claus is Going to Town On Me* under the pen name M.L. Eliza.

Originally from Bolton, UK, Marie now lives in North Carolina, USA. When she's not writing, she can usually be found playing the same three video games on a loop (*cough* Dragon Age)